"I haven't fo

with yet. Truthful settle down," Ken woman seemed nic, but she wore a reindeer headband, and Kennedy found it difficult to concentrate.

"Well, Poppy Lane isn't exactly a hotbed of activity. But you might catch the bug to settle down simply by living here. You certainly won't find a single guy, though, unless you venture off the block." The tipsy Jenny patted Kennedy's shoulder and sauntered away with the bells on her antlers jingling.

"Yeah, you might have to go to the grocery store for butter."

Upon hearing the familiar voice, Kennedy pressed a hand to her fluttering stomach and dropped her jaw. She fought to keep her smile demure and turned.

Luke grinned.

She tilted her head. "This is going to sound weird, but you are a sight for sore eyes."

He chuckled. "No weirder than the fact that you are at my boss' party."

"You mean you're at my neighborhood cookie exchange." Kennedy licked her lips and took a sip of the sugary cocktail while she inspected his party attire. She liked the way he was dressed and wondered if he struggled with deciding as she had. His quarter-zip, gray sweater and slim khakis were a perfect blend of professional and casual. Ellen would say he appeared "well put together."

Praise for Ally Hayes

"A SNOWBALL'S CHANCE was the perfect way for me to get into the Christmas spirit. Following the characters as they navigated the stress of the holidays and starting over while juggling feelings and family was so wholesome. I'd recommend it to anyone looking for a fun, flirty, festive read and who isn't scared to get their hands dirty in the process!"

~Imogen O'Reilly

~*~

"A SNOWBALL'S CHANCE might take place during a cold Midwest winter, but the story will warm your heart. Kennedy and Luke's story is a beautifully told tale of the possibilities that are out there when you open your heart up to the unknown."

~KMH, Boston

~*~

"There's nothing better than a holiday romance. Throw in some lively neighbors, a snowstorm, and Christmas cookies and you've got more than A SNOWBALL'S CHANCE of finding laughter and love in this story."

~Romance junkie in Chicago

A Snowball's Chance

by

Ally Hayes

The Christmas Cookies Series

A Snowball's Chance

Contact Information: info@thewildrosepress.com

Cover Art by *Jennifer Greef*

The Wild Rose Press, Inc.
PO Box 708
Adams Basin, NY 14410-0708
Visit us at www.thewildrosepress.com

Publishing History
First Edition, 2022
Trade Paperback ISBN 978-1-5092-4195-8
Digital ISBN 978-1-5092-4090-6

The Christmas Cookies Series
Published in the United States of America

Dedication

To my family, for always making Christmas in the Midwest special.

Chapter One

Slam. Kennedy startled awake to an ear-ringing sound of metal striking metal. *What could that be? What time is it?* She darted her hand around the nightstand until she felt the cold glass of her phone's screen and tapped it to life. *Nine already?* Kennedy never slept this late. She scanned her aunt's bedroom and reality caused her to bolt out of the unfamiliar bed.

Standing so quickly made her dizzy. She calmed her breath and reminded herself that nine o'clock here in Indiana was only six a.m. to her body clock still on California time. Adjusting to the time difference between the west coast and Indiana's eastern time zone might take a few days.

It is Sunday. I could totally go back to sleep. Kennedy turned to slide back under the covers and remembered the earsplitting sound. Recapturing sleep would be impossible.

She padded down the first few stairs, but the icy, bare wood floors sent her back to the bedroom for socks. *I'd better grab a hoodie while I'm at it since downstairs is probably even colder.* Once on the main level, she found her bearings and wove through a maze of tan moving boxes into the kitchen. In search of coffee, Kennedy explored the cabinets but gave up and settled on the first sign of caffeine—a teabag. As she filled a mug with water from the tap, she peered out the window and noticed a figure walking on the sidewalk across the street. Kennedy leaned over the stainless-steel sink to get a better view of a woman in a long, down coat and tall, furry boots. The pom-pom on top of her hat bounced with each step as she traversed from house to house, depositing papers into mailboxes.

The noise! That must have been the sound of her aunt's, or rather Kennedy's, mailbox closing. She vaguely recalled the ornate brass box mounted by the front door when she moved in yesterday. She popped her mug into the microwave, set it for two minutes, and scooted her sock-covered feet toward the foyer.

As she slid open the deadbolt, a rush of frigid air escaped the glass storm door and stung her cheeks. Kennedy pulled up the hood of her sweatshirt and braced to reach a hand into the mailbox. The sting of the cold metal reminded her to locate gloves. After retrieving a piece of red paper from the box, she lowered the lid gently to avoid a second slam and shut the front door.

Back inside, Kennedy heard the microwave's incessant beeping. Her tea was ready. While sipping, she unfolded the paper and smoothed it out on the counter. "What the…" Kennedy squinted to read the dark-green print.

Poppy Lane's Annual Cookie Exchange

Join your neighbors for some holiday cheer at Lexi and Brian's!

Saturday, December 8th

Family Fun 4-6 p.m.

Adults Only 6:30-???

Secure your sitters now, and reserve your cookie of choice by Dec. 5.

As always, bring six dozen and a box—or two!

Kennedy smirked. Surely the invitation was intended for her aunt Maggie. This Lexi somebody must not have heard she passed away.

Kennedy tossed the invitation back onto the counter. The weak tea wasn't clearing her brain fog, so she poured it down the drain and rinsed the only unpacked mug. A box labeled *Kitchen* remained unopened on the table. Unpacking wasn't high on her morning list, but some things couldn't wait. Tearing open the box, she pulled out her single-serve coffeemaker and necessary pods. Tapping a foot as the heating light turned from red to green, she picked up the invitation again.

"A cookie exchange? How 1970s." She popped in a coffee pod. As she watched the essential elixir drip into her favorite maroon-and-gold mug from college, she relaxed her shoulders.

I'll tell Mom about this when I call tonight, and we'll share a laugh. Kennedy placed the invitation on top of a pile of mail addressed to her aunt. She discovered the stack yesterday on the kitchen table, along with general house instructions. The first note read *Important* across the top in neon pink highlighter. When her coffee was ready, she carried the note and her mug over to the floral couch she mentally designated for donation.

This handwriting was very bubbly. Aunt Maggie's script was perfect, nun-taught cursive. From the list of helpful hints and tidbits, Kennedy learned the switch to the garbage disposal needed to be flicked on twice in a row to work, and the circuit box was located near the hot water tank in the basement. She assumed a lawyer or real estate agent left most of the closing documents on the table, but this note seemed more personal. Maybe Maggie's friends from her church group were responsible. They had already been very thoughtful after her aunt's passing and reached out to her family with heartfelt condolences and offers to help in any way.

Recalling her beloved great-aunt, Kennedy rubbed at the tightness in her chest.

Aunt Maggie passed away at the end of the summer. For all of Kennedy's life, Maggie lived alone in a small town in Indiana. Kennedy never visited but recalled Maggie replying to people's inquiry about her town with, "Near Muncie, but not exactly." When Kennedy was younger and researched the town on a map, she discovered Meadow Ridge appeared to be in the middle of nowhere.

Last May, Maggie had visited Kennedy's parents, Ellen and Rob, in Florida. They recently moved there from California. Until the move, Aunt Maggie would spend every Christmas with Kennedy's family, but since skipping the last holiday, none of them visited with Maggie lately. Kennedy missed her affable great-aunt and joined the reunion in Florida.

On her second day lounging by her parents' pool on a rare day off from her job at Hartley Advertising, Kennedy noticed Aunt Maggie was uncharacteristically quiet. Normally, Maggie would badger Kennedy with questions about her job, friends, and dates.

Maggie always filled them in on her bridge club, church group, and the social events of Meadow Ridge and her block of Poppy Lane.

That day, though, she thumbed through a craft

magazine and only answered direct questions with one-word answers. Eventually, she lowered the magazine, cleared her throat, and announced she had news to share. "I'm dying."

"Oh, Maggie." Ellen flapped a hand at her aunt. "You're the picture of health. No one is as active in their eighties as you."

"Nope." Maggie shook her head. "Not anymore. No, I take that back. I plan to carry on like usual until the end. Which, by the way, is in three to six months." She took a loud sip of her bright-red, strawberry daiquiri.

"Wait." Kennedy straightened in her chaise lounge. She removed her white, oval sunglasses and leaned toward her great-aunt. "Are you serious?" Her aunt was eccentric and prone to exaggeration. Kennedy loved her aunt's outlandishness and assumed the proclamation was merely another reference to growing older. Her last statement, though, struck a chord with Kennedy. Maggie sounded somber and specific. Could she be telling the truth? A wave of nausea rose in her throat.

"As serious as a heart attack, or in my case—hypertrophic cardiomyopathy." She took another slurp. "I've known for about six weeks. This is my last hurrah, at least here with you. Me and the gals are going on a cruise in July then I'll get my affairs in order when I return home. Since I don't have a husband or kids, the process should be simple. Your family and the church will get everything. Now you know." Maggie raised the magazine.

"Auntie!" Ellen grabbed Maggie's arm.

"Oh, don't go making a big fuss." Maggie shook her head. "Everyone's got to go sometime, and I'm glad for the heads-up. Not everyone gets advance notice."

"How can you be so cavalier?" Kennedy placed a hand over her chest, as if she could slow her racing heart.

"You know me. I'm a straight shooter." Maggie gun-pointed her fingers.

"Still." Ellen's voice wavered.

"Still nothing." Maggie lifted her empty glass. "Now, let's have another round and hit the casinos. Maybe I can sweeten the pot for you all."

After much protest and insistence she'd received all the second and third opinions she cared to hear, Kennedy and Ellen relented and honored all Maggie's wishes during the visit. Gambling, shopping, visiting the zoo, and swimming in the ocean were all on her to-do list. Talking about her illness was not.

On the third morning, Kennedy cornered her mom alone at the kitchen sink "Mom, I'm all for playing along, but I feel terrible and want to let her know without upsetting her."

Ellen pulled off yellow rubber gloves and sighed. "You know, words were never her strong suit. She has always expressed her love through actions and gestures. Think of all the handmade gifts she sent. I think you'll have to speak her language."

Kennedy pondered her mother's advice and struggled for a way to honor her aunt and show her affection. As the end of the weeklong visit loomed, Kennedy approached Maggie. "Auntie, I've been thinking, and I'm at a loss. Is there anything I can do for you or you want me to do before you, um, you know?"

"Before I leave this planet?" Maggie grinned and

placed a hand on Kennedy's shoulder. "Sure. Find a cute fella and settle down. Oh, and maybe go to church once in a while?"

True to her word, Aunt Maggie enjoyed a great summer with her friends, and she passed away in her sleep at the end of August. She left specific instructions for no service to be held. All her worldly possessions were left to her family and church. Kennedy and her parents were shocked to discover Kennedy inherited the house.

After taking a week to process the reality and debate the pros and cons with her family and a few close friends, Kennedy announced her plan to sell, then researched options for donating the profits. What did she need with a three-bedroom house in the Midwest suburbs? She had a life in California—an apartment, a good job, and friends. Actually, the apartment was overpriced, undersized, and in constant need of repairs. As for the job, she considered quitting every day. That just left her friends. Only one of her friends was still single; the rest were married, having kids, and moving to the suburbs themselves.

Still, 61 Poppy Lane, Meadow Ridge, Indiana was a far cry from the neighborhoods of San Francisco.

"Did Aunt Maggie really expect me to just pick up and move?" Kennedy asked her mother over the phone. "How can I at this stage?"

Ellen cleared her throat. "And what stage is that exactly?"

Kennedy shrugged. "Good question. A stagnant one."

"Well." Ellen took an audible breath. "According to the official will we received today, and you should get a copy any day now, it appears Aunt Maggie anticipated your hesitancy and gave you a caveat. She insists—and this statement is typed in bold—you stick it out for one year. The provision states she'll rest easy if you give it your best shot. If after one year on Poppy Lane you don't wish to stay, you can sell the house and do what you please with the money from the sale. It's all yours."

"Geez. She's even pushy in the afterlife." Kennedy shook her head. Laughing at Aunt Maggie felt better than the empty sensation of missing her.

After hashing out the new factor with her parents and friends, Kennedy vowed to try, and she set about making arrangements.

A waitress from her favorite coffee shop agreed to sublet her apartment. The aspiring singer and her model/actor boyfriend hoped to make it big and buy their own place by the time Kennedy returned.

As for her own career, after much deliberation, Kennedy took a leave of absence from her job as a graphic designer at the advertising agency she never meant to spend ten years at and set her sights on pursuing freelance work. A year off wouldn't be so bad, and she might gain clarity on her future career path by stepping away.

As Kennedy prepared to move, she began to look forward to the temporary change. Sometimes the fast pace of the city felt overwhelming, but the thought of fleeing for the suburbs never appealed to her. A little break might be welcome, but she'd be back. She'd never last in such a slow environment and had let her family and friends know the move was only to honor Aunt Maggie's wishes, not to settle down in the suburbs.

Now, Kennedy took another look at the invitation to the Christmas cookie exchange as evidence of the stark difference between her life in California and this stopover in Indiana. Kennedy slugged the last of her coffee and climbed the steps to get dressed for a long day of unpacking and setting up some sort of freelance website for her work. She didn't own any warm sweaters or have a need to dress up, so she selected flowered leggings and a long, gray sweatshirt. Twisting her long hair into a messy bun, she then wound a velvet scrunchie to secure the loose strands. Since she'd be lifting boxes and trudging up and down the stairs, she laced her gym shoes.

A yawn surprised her. *Maybe I should go easy on myself.* The past two days had been long ones on the road, and the time difference would affect her for the rest of Sunday. Plus, some good football games were scheduled today.

A glance at the unmade bed almost tempted her to climb back under the covers. *Ugh. If I don't start now, I'll be sleeping in Aunt Maggie's worn, pilled sheets for a year.*

Kennedy stripped the bed to replace the flannel with her own Egyptian cotton set. She carried the load to the laundry room on the first floor and stuffed everything into the washer. Another cabinet search proved fruitless. No detergent could be found. Not a single pod, drop of liquid, or trace of powder appeared to exist. She could imagine Maggie saying, "Why do laundry if I'm dying?"

"Here we go." Kennedy pulled her phone from the hidden pocket of her leggings. "Hey, Scarlett. Good morning."

"Good morning, Kennedy," the robotic voice replied. "It is Sunday, December second, and thirty-four degrees Fahrenheit with overcast skies. What can I do for you today?

"Hey, Scarlett. Start a list titled, Grocery Store, and add laundry detergent."

"Done. Anything else?"

"Oh, I'm sure there will be."

"Sorry, I didn't catch that." Scarlett's automated response triggered.

"Never mind. I mean disregard." Kennedy launched her music app and inserted her rose-gold, wireless headphones. She re-pocketed her phone and searched for the box of linens she shipped from her apartment.

By six o'clock, she was sweaty, tired, and hungry. She planned to shower, order dinner, and call her mom who would, no doubt, be waiting to hear about her moving adventure.

The shower was a pleasant surprise as water pressure was wonderful since it wasn't shared with an entire complex. Dinner from the only restaurant offering delivery on Sunday nights was mediocre. The only thing left was her scheduled phone call. Kennedy tucked into the living room's floral couch, pulled a throw pillow into her lap, and braced herself for the interrogation.

"So…" Ellen answered.

"So far, so good. You know, temporarily."

"Don't make up your mind after just one day, Ken."

Gripping the pillow, Kennedy rolled her eyes and

was glad Ellen never video chatted. "Mom, it's freezing here. No wonder Aunt Maggie always came to visit us in California for Christmas. She needed to defrost. No, this scene is not for me. Oh! You'll never believe the invitation I got in the mailbox. Not an evite. No, it was a hand-delivered computer printout. I'd say it's really more of a notice."

"Really? What is the invitation for?"

"Get this—a Christmas cookie exchange. Can you even imagine?"

"Hmm. I've never been much of a baker, but I think it sounds like fun. You should go."

Kennedy tossed the pillow to the floor. "Fun? Mom, you're kidding, right?"

"Why not? You'll meet the neighbors at least."

"I don't need to meet temporary neighbors. Plus, I think Poppy Lane's definition of fun and mine differ."

"I wouldn't be so sure about that," Ellen said. "Maggie used to mention all sorts of outings and events on the block. Give them a chance."

Just as Kennedy was about to protest, a flash lit the room. Squinting, she turned her head toward the window. From her perch on the floral couch, she could see lights shining through the large, bay window. "Maybe. Mom, I gotta go see what's going on. Poppy Lane seems to be ablaze."

"What?"

Kennedy walked toward the window and parted the sheer drapes. Thousands of twinkling lights blinded her. Another set popped on, illuminating an enormous evergreen tree. The phone slipped from her grip to the plush, mauve carpet. The impact barely made a sound.

"What is happening? Tell me!" Ellen's voice

sounded muffled from the floor.

With her left hand, Kennedy shielded her eyes and used her right to pick up the phone. “Sorry, I dropped you. The entire neighborhood appears to be simultaneously hanging Christmas lights on every surface imaginable.”

“Go out there and join in!”

“Mom! This is nuts.” Kennedy ducked behind the side, linen panel and searched for a cord to pull. “I’m closing the drapes and going upstairs to catch up on a week’s worth of our show.”

“I really think you should get out there and meet people, but go watch. I’m all caught up, and you won’t believe what Matt does next. Just promise me you’ll think about the cookie party.”

Kennedy sighed. She didn’t want to start an argument and resisted conveying her true feelings. “I will think about it, Mom. That’s all I’ll promise.”

After their goodbyes, Kennedy stole a quick glance out the window. The coast was not clear yet. From behind the veil of the curtain, she watched as families stood in packs and pointed at the decorative lights.

Do I hear singing? Are they walking from house to house admiring everyone’s handiwork? What did Maggie get me into? I really thought I could just play along with her wishes and move in undetected. I wanted to take this forced sabbatical to focus on myself and my career, not dive headfirst into suburban life. I’ve only been here twenty-four hours and already feel the pressure to join in. I’m no party-pooper, but this is crazy. No way would I willingly go to a cookie exchange with a bunch of pent-up parents, but I promised Mom. Actually, I only promised I’d think about it. Loophole found! Now I can relax.

To make a clean getaway, Kennedy crouched low and duck-walked to the stairs. She darted up and settled into bed with her laptop opened to her streaming service. The reality show she and her mother watched was anything but realistic, but compared to the show outside her window, the world of one guy dating thirty women suddenly seemed plausible.

Chapter Two

Lowering the fluffy, white comforter just below her chin, Kennedy cleared her throat. "Hey, Scarlett. Tell me about my day." She pulled the comforter to under her nose.

"Hello, Kennedy. Today is Monday, December third, and the current temperature is forty degrees with sunny skies. Today, you have grocery shopping, research, and workout. Would you like to hear your grocery list now?"

"No, thank you. Please play my wake-up songs." Bass and piano filled the air. Kennedy dozed through two songs before folding back the thick cover. She pulled her robe from the hook on the door and slid her feet into plush slippers. The chill would not shock her today.

While drinking her coffee, she scrolled through her social media feed. A photo popped up from a coworker back in San Francisco—*former coworker*? The caption read *It's beginning to look a lot like Christmas. Not!* The photo depicted felt walls half-heartedly draped with gold, foil garland.

—Ha! You should see this neighborhood at night. Like Santa's Village!—

They exchanged texts while Kennedy ate a protein bar from the bottom of her purse. The conversation made her smile for the connection but instilled guilt for not working and still lounging in her robe. Vowing to start researching later in the afternoon, she crumpled her breakfast wrapper and tossed it in the trash.

Kennedy asked Scarlett for directions to the closest store and zipped up a light-blue sweatshirt and pulled on black joggers. *Look at me. I'll fit right in with the suburban moms buying peanut butter and juice boxes.* While tying her gym shoes, she heard the doorbell. *Ugh, not now. I should install one of those doorbell cameras. Not for me, of course, but the upgrade could add market value to the house. It's probably someone selling something, so I'll just ignore it.*

Knock-knock-knock.

I'd better go see what this is all about. Kennedy finished double knotting the laces and clomped down the stairs. Through the long, rectangle windows flanking the front door, she saw a woman waving and smiling. She sported a short, blonde bob with an arrow-straight part and bright-red, long nails.

With a forced smile, Kennedy thrust her left hand to open the heavy door and propped the glass storm door with her right elbow. *Damn, that blast of air stung.* She winced instinctively then composed herself. "Hi. Can I help you?"

"Hi! I'm Lexi! Welcome, Kennedy."

Startled this stranger knew her name, Kennedy was at a loss for words.

"Lexi, you know. Your neighbor from across the street." She pointed behind her. "I'm the one who dropped off the invitation. I wanted to make sure you got it. After noticing your lights on yesterday, I figured you'd finally moved in. Actually, I delivered them to everyone else two weeks ago, but I dropped off gentle reminders yesterday to those I hadn't heard from." Lexi cocked her head. Her hair barely moved.

"Oh." Kennedy blinked several times while she deciphered the fast-talking woman's announcement. "Would you like to come in?" Recalling the crumpled invitation on the kitchen counter, she immediately regretted the offer.

Lexi waved her right hand. "No, no. I was only stopping by to say hi and make sure you'll be there. I've got you down for snowball cookies—of course."

Of course? What does she mean? "Um, okay." Kennedy forced a smile to hide her confusion.

"Well, you look like you're heading to work out, and I'm staging an open house in twenty, so I'll let you go."

"Okay. Thanks for stopping by."

Lexi shot out her arm and kept the glass door open. "Wait. Um, not to be too forward or anything, but I assume you noticed the block decorated last night? Well, it's kind of a tradition around here. I tried to call last night, but I guess the phone has been shut off. I'm sure there's a box somewhere with Maggie's lights and displays. She always participated—big time. I'm not saying decorating is mandatory, but you know."

Oh, boy. Kennedy grinned and nodded. "I got it. And yeah, I had the phone service disconnected. I've never actually had a landline."

Lexi's eyes widened. "Let me know if you need any help. You've got my cell number on the invitation. Toodles!"

Kennedy allowed the storm door to slam but hesitated to close the main door. Through the glass, she watched Lexi exit.

Hopping down the front steps, she then climbed the running board to her huge, white SUV. She popped on mirrored sunglasses and waggled her fingers as she backed away.

Kennedy felt her cheeks redden at being caught watching. She closed the door and shook her head. *Great. Not only do I have to learn how to make snowball cookies and attend a party, but now I also have to hang outdoor Christmas lights.*

"Hey, Scarlett, how do you make snowball cookies?"

"I found a recipe on the Internet. Would you like me to read it to you?"

"No. Please add the ingredients to my grocery shopping list."

"Done."

Mom would be mortified.

Ellen always prepared a handwritten list organized by category. She even carried a pen in her purse and crossed off items as she shopped. She never seemed in a hurry or frustrated.

Kennedy, on the other hand, was usually rushed and preferred a digital version instead of wasting paper. But she sometimes felt foolish staring at her phone as she zipped through the aisles. One more time, she perused her list on her phone before slipping on the new, puffy jacket her friends gave her as a going-away present. "It's only one winter," Kennedy had said at the makeshift party. "But I do love it." She hugged the jacket to her chest, then embraced each friend as they had shared drinks at a local gastro pub.

Now, the silver-and-black, shiny nylon and down jacket was a welcome necessity. Shivering in her car and blasting the heater were new experiences. The car's onboard GPS system guided her to the enormous parking lot of the closest grocery store. Back in California, she was used to small, specialty shops and ordered most of her staples online. Brick-and-mortar stores like the Meadow Ridge Mart were a bit outside of her comfort zone.

Kennedy took a breath and walked through the automatic doors and toward the green shopping carts. After filling her cart with laundry detergent and softener, coffee, protein bars, and frozen lean entrees, she realized she might need more substantial groceries. *Should I buy fresh fruit and vegetables? I'm so used to having lunch, and often dinners, at work or out with friends. What will I do now? Could I make the salads and wraps I usually picked up on my lunch break? Maybe a place is nearby to order lunch. I can't think about that now. I have a mission.* Kennedy steered down the dairy aisle.

A display for cookie dough prestamped with Christmas trees made her smile. Slice and bake was more her speed. The familiar rolls sat next to her favorite brand of avocado butter.

"Right, cookies." Kennedy tapped her phone. "Hey, Scarlett, what are the ingredients for snowball cookies?" As soon as she finished the request, she cringed. She recalled the TV commercial poking fun at people who use the speaker function in stores.

"Okay, here are the ingredients for snowball cookies, according to Best Recipe dot com: one cup butter, one-fourth cup sugar, one teaspoon vanilla extract, two cups all-purpose flour, two cups finely chopped pecans, and powdered sugar."

"Whoa."

Kennedy heard a voice say followed by a chuckle. A male chuckle.

Her stomach dropped, and she prepared to apologize for the volume, but when she turned her head, she lost her voice. Before her stood a guy around her age holding a handbasket. He wore a navy, wool pea coat. Brown leather gloves protruded from the pockets. Her cheeks burned.

He smiled and held up a hand. "Sorry, I wasn't laughing at you. Well, not exactly."

"Oh," Kennedy said. "Were the eggs cracking jokes?"

"Funny," he said. "You know, dairy jokes."

Slapping a palm to her forehead, she groaned.

The guy laughed.

"So, what *was* so funny?"

"I think we're in the same bind." He held up his phone.

The screen read: *Two large eggs, one-half cup of unsalted butter, two cups sugar, one cup heavy cream.*

Kennedy laughed, then bunched her eyebrows.

"What?" He tilted his head. "You appear baffled."

"Mine just says butter. Yours says unsalted butter. Is there a difference? Is it important?"

"I have no clue." The guy pointed at Kennedy's phone. "Wanna ask your friend?"

"Scarlett? She prefers her professional title—virtual assistant."

He snickered. "My apologies, Scarlett. Why Scarlett? Like the actress?"

"No, like O'Hara. My favorite literary character." Kennedy waved her free hand. "It's a long story."

"You're right. That is a very long book."

"Ugh!" She put a palm to her forehead again.

"Yes? Can I help you with something?" the voice from the phone asked.

"Oops, must've hit the home button." Kennedy posed the butter question, and Scarlett explained the pros and cons of salt content. Kennedy stole glances as he listened and nodded.

He was definitely attractive. His clean-shaven face and close-cropped hair created a look she found appealing. So many guys her age sported beards, and she was tired of the so-called rugged appearance. His eyes were light, but Kennedy couldn't tell if they were green or blue. Either way, she liked the way they contrasted with his dark hair. She had always wished her own brown eyes didn't match her brown hair. Rather than resorting to colored contacts, she opted for golden highlights. Instinctively, she touched her hair.

He lifted his head.

Heat crept to her face once again.

"Well, I need to find the rest of these ingredients. Please thank Scarlett for me."

"I would, but I don't know your name," Kennedy said. The sudden boldness surprised her, but she felt oddly comfortable flirting with this stranger. In California, she was constantly on guard and never made the first move. All dating was initiated from the safe distance of a phone app.

The guy blushed but smirked. "Luke." He extended a hand.

As she shook his warm hand, she grinned, her body temperature soaring. "You know Scarlett, but I'm Kennedy."

"Nice learning about butter with you, Kennedy."

"Yes. Who knew? Actually, I'll bet most people do know. Oh, well, now we do, too." She recognized her nervous ramble and pursed her lips.

"Best of baking luck." Luke turned and rounded the corner, out of view.

"You, too," Kennedy shouted to an empty aisle.

Luke leaned back so only his head appeared, then waved. He offered a wide smile—complete with dimples.

Kennedy stared at the butter and egg display for a full minute. "Hey, Scarlett?" she whispered. "What just happened?"

****

Back at the house, Kennedy held open the refrigerator door with her hip while she arranged the eggs, almond milk, butter, yogurt, and fruit. The door had a mind of its own and slammed shut every time she let go, but sometimes it did not close all the way when she actually tried. Another repair. Yesterday, she discovered the dryer squeaked. Oh, the joys of homeownership.

Ding. "Reminder—it is noon, and you have research scheduled."

"I'll start after lunch," she called as if her virtual assistant was an actual person. "Hey, Scarlett, how do I store flour and sugar by the pound?"

"In a sealed, cool, dry place."

Kennedy spun around the kitchen. Vowing to attempt the recipe the next day, she stuffed the ingredients in a corner cabinet and powered up her laptop. Seated at the worn, kitchen table, Kennedy began what she hoped would launch the next phase of her career.

She truly loved being a graphic artist, but she no longer enjoyed working from eight in the morning to whenever her boss left. The firm expanded every year, and while the growth proved positive at the onset, recently the size seemed more of a negative. Grateful for an offer right after college, Kennedy joined Hartley without hesitation. At first, she was happy to learn the ropes as an assistant and thrilled to eventually earn her own accounts. Ten years later, she boasted four exclusive clients and a handful of occasional accounts.

Still, she believed her creativity was often stifled. Her clients had their set ideas and were unreceptive to change. Kennedy experienced this frustrating situation with her boss as well. Recently, she pitched some innovative ideas which were immediately rejected. She was fed up and ready to call the shots, but at the time, she hadn't known how to proceed.

When the move to Indiana popped up, so did the issue of her career's future. Kennedy turned to her father for advice. Rob was an accountant who worked at the same firm for forty years before retiring. She wondered if he ever thought of leaving or if he considered his daughter crazy for deserting a stable position.

"Going off on your own at this point is a great move, honey," Rob told Kennedy. "It's also risky, so I suggest a safety net. Taking a leave of absence, rather than completely quitting, gives you some leeway, and the move explains the timing to your bosses." Her dad lived his life cautiously and always appeared happy and successful, so she had heeded his advice.

Now, while staring at her computer screen, she

stood at ground zero. Not only would she have to learn how to market herself, but she also needed to learn the freelance market. First, she needed to establish a presence with a website. Kennedy sighed. At least she knew how to begin and the amount of time and effort it would require—a lot. Designing a website was one thing, but maintaining it and turning a profit would prove a challenge. Thankfully, all the programs necessary to start today's task were already loaded on her laptop. "Hey, Scarlett. Play work tunes."

Early 2000s pop music filled the air as Kennedy tapped and clicked. She adjusted fonts and colors, uploaded photos, and experimented with banners. Two hours elapsed when Scarlett reminded her to stretch. Kennedy rose and lifted her arms above her head and rolled her neck.

Back at the office, she would've visited her coworkers for a break, so instead, she strolled the house and assessed her aunt's décor. The striped wallpaper and heavy drapes would need to go before listing. She navigated through the maze of boxes toward the dining room. Along with her own boxes were various bins, containers, even shopping bags, filled with Maggie's possessions. Her church friends packed everything except the furniture, and when they heard Maggie's niece was moving in, they left the boxes for Kennedy to decide what should be kept or donated. The task seemed daunting, so she continued toward the dining room, but a box labeled Outdoor Christmas Decorations blocked the entrance.

Ugh. Kennedy retreated toward the front of the house and peered out the bay window. The sun was fading. Everyone else's lights would be coming on soon. *Should I get out there now? What do I even do? Where do I start? Darkness will fall in just over an hour. Is it even worth it?*

"Time to get back to work," Scarlett announced.

"That answers that." Kennedy closed the drape and retreated. Back at the kitchen table, she typed away while the colored lights of Poppy Lane began to shine through her windows.

Great. Nothing like twinkly guilt. Tomorrow, I promise.

After another hour of work, she took a break to check her social media accounts. She replied to a few friends, returned a streak of selfies, and shared GIFs. Getting back to work, she opened her bulletin board app, intending to create a new board for her yet-unnamed freelance business, and she noticed three new "Ideas for You" notifications and tapped the icon.

The best snowball cookie recipe ever!

Perfect snowballs for the perfect Christmas!

Easy-peasy snowballs.

"What the…" Kennedy said. "How did it know?" Shaking her head and wondering for the millionth time if she relied too heavily on Scarlett, Kennedy clicked on the easy recipe. At first glance, it looked simple enough, so she saved the link. Vowing to return to the recipe, she refocused on work. At seven, she snapped shut the laptop and tossed a lean meal-for-one in the microwave. "Hey, Scarlett. Please dial Mom."

"I hear your microwave beeping. Please tell me you are at least using a real dish," Ellen said.

"Of course." Wincing, Kennedy peeled the film from the plastic container. The dishes—and glasses and silverware—were still in boxes.

"So, how is suburbia?"

"You'd be proud of me. I went grocery shopping today and met a new neighbor." Kennedy speared an artichoke. An image of Luke popped into her head. *Wow, that had happened today, too.* She smiled.

"Well, aren't you Miss Domestication? Next, you'll be—I don't know, going to a cookie exchange?"

"Oh, please. Don't remind me." Her smile morphed into a frown. Dread set in, but she kept her voice chipper. "I did buy all the ingredients, though. This morning, I was accosted by the neighbor hosting the party. Also, I am apparently supposed to decorate. You know, colored lights on the bushes, wreaths, and all that. What did Maggie get me into?" A silence followed, and then Kennedy heard Ellen clear her throat.

"Dad and I have been talking, and we think you should embrace the whole package. Go to the cookie party, decorate outside, and maybe even put up a Christmas tree. Then, as a reward for making the effort, fly down here where the only indication it's Christmas is the Santa at the mall wearing board shorts."

Kennedy laughed. "Tempting. Let me think about it."

"Fair enough, but don't take too long. Plane fares will only increase."

Hmm. Maybe escaping for the holiday will power me through cookie parties and decorating for the next few weeks. "Thank you. I'll research my travel options."

"Great. Anything else exciting happen?"

"Nope." Heat spread across her face.

After returning wishes of love to her mom,

Kennedy allowed her mind to replay the encounter with Luke. *Sure, I liked getting attention from a cute guy, and we shared a funny moment. But really, it was nothing. The whole thing was less than five minutes. He probably forgot all about it by now, and I should, too. I'm not staying here. What's the point of making a connection? I might as well book a flight for Christmas now to avoid any further invitations or obligations. Still, those eyes.* "Hey, Scarlett. Search flights to Naples, Florida."

Chapter Three

"Need any help?"

Kennedy straightened and searched for the source of the young voice. True to her word, and with a gentle reminder from Scarlett, she began her day on Tuesday searching for Maggie's outdoor Christmas decorations. After locating the plastic boxes, she bundled up and carried everything outside. Not long after, she realized the task would be monumental and lengthy. The mess of lights she untangled and arranged on the shrubs had a cord too short to reach the single outlet by the front door. Despite many attempts at reconfiguration, the plug still hung eighteen inches shy of its destination. The voice grew louder and closer.

"You need an extension cord."

The sun was bright, and she had to squint to detect a mitten-clad hand waving from the sidewalk. She beckoned the boy to her yard.

"Hi. I'm Caleb." The teenage boy wore a blue, fleece jacket, and his hands were hooked under the straps of an overstuffed, black backpack.

Kennedy pointed at his bag. "Wow. I must have lost track of time. Is it after school already?"

"Nah." Caleb shook his head. "Final exams start next week, so we have half days this week to study. It's only lunchtime now."

"Oh, sorry. I must seem nuts. I'm Kennedy, and

I'm a bit in over my head here. I'm from California and lived in an apartment my entire adult life, so this is all new for me." She pointed toward the lights and decorations strewn about the lawn.

"California?" Caleb's eyes widened. "Sweet. This must be like a total culture shock. Don't get me wrong. I love it here. Poppy Lane is cool and all, but not every block is as, um, into decorating as we are. Actually, I heard the lady who used to live here was kind of responsible."

"My aunt Maggie? Really?" A pang of chest constriction caught Kennedy off guard. Was this guilt for hesitating to decorate or sentimentality for her aunt? Now that she thought about it, of course Maggie would have embraced decorating. Celebrations and festivities were totally her thing. Maggie would've loved to see Kennedy untangling the lights. She forced her quivering lips into a tight line.

"That's what I was told." Caleb lowered his head and shuffled his feet. "I knew her my whole life. She was awesome. I'm sorry she passed away."

"Thanks. Yeah, she was my fave." Kennedy sensed tears brimming and took a deep breath to keep them at bay. "So, what am I missing?"

Laughing, Caleb dropped his backpack on the flagstone walkway. "Where's the box?"

Two hours later, Caleb walked home—two doors down—after hanging her lights, arranging electrical cords, and setting timers. He also showed her the online listing for a local sub and salad shop and downloaded the app to order lunch.

Kennedy insisted on treating for all his help and sacrificing study time.

"No worries." Caleb hoisted his backpack over one shoulder. "I probably would've played video games anyway, and I'm always happy to help. Call me anytime to like shovel or mow. I'll do just about anything. I'm saving to buy a cool car. Mom's minivan isn't going to cut it next year when I'm a senior."

Kennedy laughed. This kid appeared capable of manual labor and lifting her spirits. "I'm sure I will have plenty of chores for you. Snow removal didn't even occur to me."

Caleb grinned. "Leave it to me. I'm your guy, Ms. Moore."

After waving goodbye, Kennedy sighed. *My guy. I move to suburbia, and now, my guy is a sixteen-year-old looking to make a buck. No, I am grateful. He seems like a good kid, and I certainly need his help. But a guy? Luke from the grocery store is more my type—and my age! Whatever. I'm not here for love, but I'm just stuck here out of love for Maggie and her crazy wishes.* Kennedy dragged the empty boxes into the garage and steered her thoughts back to work.

****

By Thursday, Kennedy felt more grounded. Thanks to Caleb, her yard lit up every night at five on the dot. A giant wreath with a red, velvet bow adorned her front door courtesy of the fourth-grade girl who lived next door.

Amelia sold the monstrosity to Kennedy as part of a fundraiser for her scout troop and informed Kennedy she'd be back in February for a cookie order.

The main floor remained crammed full of boxes, but Kennedy unpacked all her clothes and placed everything in drawers and hung her nicer outfits in the closet. She wondered how long it would be before she would wear those work staples again. For the fourth day in a row, she sported an oversized sweatshirt and leggings. “Hey, Scarlett, real pants tomorrow.”

“Okay. I put real pants on your schedule.”

Pathetic. Kennedy rolled her eyes.

She intended to try the recipe on Thursday. She really did, but by noon she was on a roll creating her website and inserting eye-catching examples of her work. In the late afternoon, she got an idea to not only set up a virtual design studio but also to transform one of the upstairs rooms into an office and physical studio. A designated space away from the coffee maker and refrigerator might prove more productive. Also, her back was sore from sitting on the kitchen set’s pine, lattice-backed chair. A rolled towel for lumbar support helped, but she still often found the need to stretch.

Kennedy saved her latest design and ventured upstairs. Next to the master bedroom she used was a smaller bedroom. Twin beds with a nightstand between them, two dressers, and a bookcase filled the space. No desk. She guessed, since no kids grew up in the house, this must have been used as a guest room. Back when she was a little girl, Kennedy would have loved to stay in this room and now wondered if anyone ever did. *Maybe Maggie intended to have kids someday. Maybe she hoped I would fill this room with my own.* Kennedy shook her head to clear the thought. She wasn’t staying, and too much furniture would have to be moved to make this room into an office. She closed the door halfway.

The final room upstairs was next to the bathroom. Prior to moving in, Ellen informed Kennedy it was

Aunt Maggie's sewing room. During the move, Kennedy briefly peered inside, but she had yet to truly inspect the space. The door creaked as she pushed it. A sewing machine/table combo stood prominently against the window facing the deep backyard. Kennedy was delighted to see the chair was a modern, desk type and could be raised and lowered, swiveled, and tilted. A banquet-sized folding table ran the length of the longer wall. Several round, white laundry baskets filled with material stood under the table. A wide closet filled the other, shorter wall. Bracing herself, she opened the squeaky, bi-fold doors and was relieved to discover the closet was empty. The final wall with the entry door was bare and boasted cheery, yellow paint. The glossy finish aided reflection from the light of the overhead ceiling fan. This must have been where Maggie made all her crafts. Kennedy recalled the many handmade dolls and accessories she received from her aunt and felt a wash of guilt. "Hey, Scarlett. Text Mom."

—Would it be wrong to turn Aunt Maggie's sewing room into an office?—

—Why would you think that?—

—Seems like a shrine.—

—She'd want you to use it for your own creativity.—

—Thanks, Mom. U da best.—

The room grew dark, and Kennedy's stomach grumbled, but she was determined to start the transformation. She turned on the overhead light and continued measuring and rearranging the sewing room to suit her style. Finally, over another microwaved meal, she searched online and ordered fake, succulent plants and tasteful prints to adorn the walls and her makeshift desk. To conduct virtual interviews with clients, she needed to appear professional and impressive. Her work would speak for itself, but some clients wanted the human connection. Eventually, she plopped into bed with an e-book about women entrepreneurs. “Hey, Scarlett, remind me to bake snowballs tomorrow and then play yacht rock for twenty minutes.”

On Friday morning, Kennedy woke with a sense of dread and wondered if it was too late to back out of the party. *No, canceling is wrong, and really, what else do I have this weekend? Plus, Ellen will ask. It’s only a bunch of cookies. I’ll bring them over, meet a few neighbors, and sneak out. I’m not looking to make friends, but I do resolve to be friendly. By this time next year, someone else will receive the invitation while I’m warm and tan in California. No worries.*

After a workout and a few hours at the computer, Kennedy pulled all the ingredients from the cabinets and refrigerator.

Step-by-step, Scarlett described the process.

Sounds easy enough. This shouldn’t take too long. While rolling the concoction into balls, though, producing a sphere proved impossible. Crumbling ensued, powdered sugar stuck to her fingers, and none of the balls turned out the same size, shape, or color. *Oh well. Maybe they will even out in the baking process.* She popped them inside the preheated oven and set about cleaning the mess.

“Hey, Ms. Moore! It’s me, Caleb,” a muffled voice delivered.

Kennedy gazed out the kitchen window and spotted Caleb shivering on her front walk. She motioned for him to meet her at the front door and hurried to open it. "It's freezing. Come on inside."

"Nah." Caleb stuck out his foot to prop the door. "My boots are all wet. It's like snow-raining. Yuck."

"Oh, I hadn't noticed." Kennedy peered behind him and saw the annoying precipitation. "What can I do for you?"

"It's supposed to snow for real this weekend. Want me to shovel? I'm going around to everyone so I can figure out a schedule." He held up his phone, revealing a mini spreadsheet.

"Sure. How does twenty dollars sound?" Realizing she had no idea if she offered too little or too much, Kennedy winced. She didn't want to seem rude, or worse—ignorant. "Is that a good amount? Again, this is new territory." She hoped his smile meant she guessed well.

"That's awesome. Thanks." He tapped his phone and nodded. "I got you in."

"Thanks, Caleb."

"See you later." He began to close the door, then turned back and pointed. "Wait. I think something is burning inside."

"Snowballs! OMG!" Kennedy let the door slam and ran for the kitchen. Smoke hung in the air. She grabbed an oven mitt and pulled out the ruined cookies. A quick inspection confirmed brown tops and black bottoms. They looked nothing like snowballs. She slid the parchment paper into the trash can, flung the oven mitt, and dropped into a chair at the kitchen table. The invitation lay in the middle of the table, taunting her. A sick feeling formed in the pit of her stomach.

Six dozen. She'd forgotten about the amount. *I*

guess I would've had to go to the store again anyway. Good thing I don't have plans tonight. Kennedy snorted. Months had passed since her last date. Labor Day weekend was her official, final foray with online dating. After one too many disasters, near misses, and no-shows, she determined a change was necessary. After deleting all the apps from her phone and laptop, she felt a huge weight lift. The house became hers a month later, and the move and career change consumed the fall months. While Kennedy didn't miss the stress of swiping and sweating, having a reason to dress in real clothes on a Friday night might be nice. A restaurant or bar would be a welcome end to the week. She sighed. Tonight, the grocery store would have to suffice. For a laugh, she changed into jeans and applied mascara.

During the drive, the weather worsened.

Kennedy was freezing and soaked by the time she entered the store. At the entrance, she shook her wet hair and grunted as she pried a black, plastic basket from the stack. She grabbed more flour, sugar, and pecans from the baking aisle and wove her way toward dairy. The basket handle dug into her arm, and she hoped not much more would need to be added. "Hey, Scarlett, how much butter is needed for six dozen cookies?"

Scarlett's reply was drowned out by a chuckle—a familiar chuckle. Her heart fluttered, and she turned her head slowly while silently hoping the voice belonged to Luke. Upon discovering him, she fought to hide a smile.

"You and Scarlett having a fun Friday night at the grocery store?"

"At least I have Scarlett." She pointed to his empty hand. "Where's your hot date?"

Luke laughed and pulled his phone from his coat pocket. "Mine is the standard robotic, factory-installed voice. But it is female."

Kennedy rolled her eyes. "So basic." She smoothed her hair and tucked a wet strand behind her ear.

"So, back for more?" Luke took a step closer and tapped the basket in her hand.

"Literally," Kennedy replied. "You, too?" Her pulse raced.

"I only stopped in on my way home from work for a few basics. I gave up on making anything for my boss' party." He shrugged. "I'll probably bring a growler of beer."

Luke is speaking my language. I like him even more now. Not only does he have amazing eyes and good hair, despite the weather, but he also seems so chill. She nodded. "I like your plan. I wish I could copy it, but I have a very important cookie assignment. I'm much better at beer, though."

Shuffling his feet, Luke cleared his throat. "Glad to hear it, because the brewery I planned to get it from is not too far. Any chance you can get away from baking and join me for a drink?"

Kennedy blushed. *Is he reading my mind? I want to drop this basket and hug him. I have to play this cool, though.* "I'd really love to, but I have to make six dozen cookies, and I ruined my first attempt. Can I take a rain check?"

"Only if I can take your number. If Scarlett allows that, of course."

"She's not the boss." Kennedy snickered and

recited her number. A second later, her phone pinged, and the message from Luke bore an umbrella and checkmark emoji. She added him as a contact and replied with a smiley face and a mug of beer.

"Cool." Luke grinned.

Kennedy smiled and reached in front of him for two cartons of eggs and stole a peek at his eyes. They were definitely green—and amazing.

Later, as she spent the next four hours attempting the second, so-called easy-peasy recipe, thoughts of Luke consumed her. Kennedy wondered if he was from Meadow Ridge and what he did for work. Her good mood required good tunes, and she selected a dance playlist and moved with a new lightness around the kitchen. She almost tuned to a Christmas songs channel on her radio app but figured it was bad enough she wore Maggie's Mrs. Claus apron. *I've only got a snowball's chance in hell at pulling this off anyway. They'd better work out this time and be worth turning down a hot guy and a night at a brewery with people my own age.*

She wasn't feeling up for a talk with her mom and realized it was after midnight anyway, so she sent a short text.

—Time got away from me with all the baking. I'll call you tomorrow after I escape the "party"—

Chapter Four

Kennedy arranged her hair into a high ponytail, and she descended the stairs. She'd overslept, but plenty of time remained for a long run before getting ready for the party. Yawning, she padded into the kitchen and poured water into the coffee maker. Six dozen, give or take a few, semi-round, powdered-sugar-covered blobs adorned the countertops of the kitchen. The sweet smell of warm sugar lingered.

"Good enough," Kennedy said out loud. Ample time existed for another attempt, but she did not have the confidence they would look any better. *I'll simply box them up like Lexi indicated and get on with my day. No one is expecting anything from me anyway. No one will ever really get to know me.*

While the coffeepot hummed to life, Kennedy entered the attached garage where she stored the empty moving and delivery boxes. She hadn't broken down the boxes for recycling since they would be needed for the return move. The garage had more than enough room for her compact car and the detritus. A medium-sized box bearing the insignia of a popular online retailer would do the trick. Several boxes from the distributor arrived recently as she set up her new office/studio and ordered warm clothes. Back inside, she drained her first cup of coffee and lined the box with the last of the parchment paper from Friday night's baking. While stacking the snowballs inside, powdered sugar scattered like glitter, and a few of the cookies crumbled.

I hope this isn't some kind of contest. If so, I've got a snowball's chance in hell at achieving honorable mention. With the cookies packed, Kennedy dressed for her long run, as was her usual Saturday routine for the past few years. On her last Saturday run by the bay, she wore only a tank and shorts. Today's run required a few more layers. "Hey, Scarlett. Start my five-mile playlist." She pushed her head through a white, mock turtleneck.

"Sure. Don't forget the cookie exchange party at six-thirty tonight."

"How could I forget?" Finally, she pulled on the running gloves she'd received in the mail yesterday and set out to discover her new, but temporary, route. Running in the cold didn't sound appealing, but she could endure it for a couple of months. *At least my knees might enjoy the flat, midwestern roads as a break from the San Francisco hills. Maybe living in Meadow Ridge does have a benefit.* Kennedy popped in her earbuds. "We shall see."

****

At six twenty-five, a soft chime echoed throughout the bedroom.

"Hey, Scarlett, cancel the reminder." Kennedy stood before her open closet. *I'll be fashionably late. Now I have to figure out what is fashionable for this soiree.*

Blouses and leather pants, a brown suede skirt, a cream sweater, and even the dress she only wore to church were strewn over her bed. Still at a loss, she texted her mom to ask her opinion.

—Whatever you feel good in. If you don't like what you're wearing, you won't feel confident.—

—You're right. As always. Thx—

—Keep me updated.—

—Thumbs-up emoji—

Kennedy lifted a thin, black, V-neck, cashmere sweater from a drawer and plucked dark, high-rise jeans from a hanger. She tugged on tall, black, suede boots and nodded at her reflection in the full-length mirror. A few, simple accessories would complete the look.

Satisfied with her appearance and slightly less satisfied with her cookie contribution, Kennedy crossed Poppy Lane. As she approached Lexi's house, she could hear the commotion from inside. Kennedy took a deep breath and rang the doorbell.

A boy of about ten years old with a blond, asymmetrical haircut answered the door. "I'm Todd. The coat taker." He thrust out his arms.

"Hi there, Todd. I'm Kennedy Moore, the new neighbor." She shrugged off her coat and laid it across his outstretched arms.

Todd spun on his heels. "Mom! The new lady is here."

Here we go. It's too late to turn around now, so I will fake having fun until I can make my getaway. With sweaty hands, Kennedy gripped the box of cookies.

"Coming!" Lexi's voice filled the foyer.

Kennedy remembered to hold her head high and smile.

"Merry Christmas," Lexi called as she approached.

Her silver high heels clacked on the tile floor. Her sleeveless, red, velvet sheath dress clung to her perfect figure.

With her free arm, she hugged Kennedy while the other lifted a flute of champagne. “Cheers to adult time.”

“Oh, right.” Kennedy nodded, recalling the invitation and offered the box. “Here are the snowballs. I’m afraid they aren’t much to look at…”

Lexi waved the air. “Oh shush, you. Knowing your aunt, I’m sure they are perfect.” She took the box and scrunched her face. “I guess you haven’t had a chance to fully unpack yet.”

Unsure how her neighbor knew she wasn’t settled in yet, Kennedy searched for a vague answer to avoid a lengthy discussion about her temporary living situation. “Yeah. I’m not sure I ever will. It’s kind of a long story.”

“Well, I’d love to hear it another time. Let’s take a peek.” Lexi peered into the box and widened her eyes. She folded the box’s flaps over the contents. “I’ll just put these down for now while we get you a drink. I’ll plate them in a bit. Follow me.”

What the? Should I be offended or relieved? Now, I’m just confused. Kennedy followed Lexi past a massive dining room adorned with a modern chandelier hanging over a twenty-foot glass table. Cookies of all shapes and sizes—frosted, sprinkled, and even three-dimensional—were displayed on china and crystal plates and platters. The dishes filled the table and matching buffet tucked along the wall. *Aha. Mine are not quite up to par.*

“Let’s go out back to the three-season room where we’ve set up the bar and appetizers.” Lexi pointed toward the rear of the house.

Kennedy followed her hostess and watched with mouth agape as Lexi leaned into a butler's pantry and swiftly deposited the cookies onto a counter next to bags of chips and open boxes of crackers. Out of the corner of her eye, she spied another cast-off contribution. *No, it can't be the same. This growler has to be a coincidence.* Kennedy let Lexi go ahead, and she stepped back to get a closer look at the growler.

"No." Kennedy smacked a hand over her mouth and gazed around to see if anyone heard. The party noise was a pleasant level of chitchat and music. She hoped the din covered her gasp and escaped to the glassed-in room.

Lexi reappeared carrying a fancy, stemmed glass filled with sparkling, pink liquid. Three cranberries floated amidst foam on top. "This year's signature drink—Lexi's Lightning." She extended the glass.

"It looks quite festive." She lifted the glass to her lips and sipped. She fought a wince as the sweetness hit her tongue.

Flashing a tight smile, Lexi grabbed Kennedy's elbow. "C'mon into the living room and meet everyone."

Kennedy allowed herself to be pulled into a room furnished with plush, rose-gold sofas, herringbone wing chairs, and marble coffee and end tables. The soft gray-and-white, papered walls featured oil paintings of Lexi, her husband, and young son and daughter. The family appeared to be posing in the middle of a field of tall grass.

"Everyone," Lexi announced. "This is our newest addition to Poppy Lane. Meet Kennedy Moore."

A short brunette stepped forward. "Hi, Kennedy.

I'm Marci from the corner. This is my husband, Jeff." She pointed to a balding guy holding a plate of shrimp cocktail.

Next, a blonde wearing a sparkly dress waved from her position by the fireplace. "I'm Tamra. I live diagonal from you in the red brick house."

"So nice to meet all of you." Kennedy offered a wide wave. She hoped the blanket greeting would halt the individual introductions.

Lexi placed a hand on Kennedy's arm. "I'm sure you'll get to know everyone eventually."

"Thanks. I'm sure I will." Kennedy shot a brief smile and continued to scan the room for the one person she did want to know. *Luke isn't here. Of course, he's not. The growler means nothing. Anyone can bring beer. Beer is a normal party contribution. Maybe not at a cookie exchange, though? No, stop being stupid.*

An hour seemed like a polite amount of time to stay. With a quick glance at her phone, she began the countdown in her head. She chatted with a few people, including a couple sporting matching, ugly Christmas sweaters. Kennedy answered the standard questions about her job, hometown, college, and predictably—her dating status. Everyone knew someone she should meet. Caleb's mother, Jenny, was especially interested and grilled Kennedy on why such a pretty girl was single.

"I haven't found the person I want to settle down with yet. Truthfully, I never had the desire to actually settle down," Kennedy told Jenny. The fortysomething woman seemed nice, but she wore a reindeer headband, and Kennedy found it difficult to concentrate.

"Well, Poppy Lane isn't exactly a hotbed of

activity. But you might catch the bug to settle down simply by living here. You certainly won't find a single guy, though, unless you venture off the block." The tipsy Jenny patted Kennedy's shoulder and sauntered away with the bells on her antlers jingling.

"Yeah, you might have to go to the grocery store for butter."

Upon hearing the familiar voice, Kennedy pressed a hand to her fluttering stomach and dropped her jaw. She fought to keep her smile demure and turned.

Luke grinned.

She tilted her head. "This is going to sound weird, but you are a sight for sore eyes."

He chuckled. "No weirder than the fact that you are at my boss' party."

"You mean you're at my neighborhood cookie exchange." Kennedy licked her lips and took a sip of the sugary cocktail while she inspected his party attire. She liked the way he was dressed and wondered if he struggled with deciding as she had. His quarter-zip, gray sweater and slim khakis were a perfect blend of professional and casual. Ellen would say he appeared "well put together."

"How about neither of us is here, and we go check out the brewery? I believe you owe me a rain check." He tapped her glass. "Unless, of course, you'd rather stay and enjoy Lexi's Lightning?"

Kennedy leaned to her right and placed the drink on the coffee table. She waved a hand toward the large bay window facing the front yard where fat snowflakes could be seen falling in the light of Lexi's front yard display. "Snow check."

"Close enough." Luke offered his arm.

The excitement of touching Luke made Kennedy blush, but she linked her arm through his and shuffled among the party guests out to the hallway dividing the living and dining rooms.

People congregated around the large table and pointed at cookies.

"We'd better make a run for it before the judging," Kennedy said.

"Is there really a contest?" Luke asked.

"I honestly don't know, but I do know judgments will be made." Kennedy smirked.

He shook his head. "We can't leave before I see your creation. Scarlett and I were essential parts of the process."

Kennedy laughed. "My snowballs are easy to find. They were banished to the pantry right next to your contribution."

Cocking his head, he set his brows.

Kennedy squeezed his arm. "You'll see. Over here." She guided him toward the narrow room. She poked her head into the pantry and motioned for Luke to follow.

Luke gripped the door frame, peered into the space, and groaned. "At least we were both exiled. Further evidence we should leave."

"And I see coats. Bonus." Kennedy pointed to a rolling rack at the back of the pantry.

Luke helped Kennedy slip on her jacket and led her toward the foyer. At the front door, Luke hesitated. "I thought I might want an easy exit, so I drove here and parked on the street. We could order a car, though, so we can let loose."

"Sounds good to me. I always had the easy way

out. I walked across the street."

"Cool." Luke opened his rideshare app. "I'll order one and give Scarlett a break. I mean, I really should put some effort into this since it's been effortless so far."

"Seriously." Kennedy took a deep breath to calm her racing heart. "I think we've been very fortunate, and ignoring karma at this point would be rude." She lowered her voice. "I do feel a bit bad ducking out of the party." *I really want to be alone with him, but I don't want to seem like a flake. I'll have to keep it light and fun to pull off this getaway. We seem to have the same sense of humor and ideas of fun, and these coincidences are making me think I would be nuts to pass up this opportunity.*

"Hey, we can stay if you want to see how your cookies stack against those inferior versions I saw in the dining room."

"No way. Mine have about a snowball's chance in hell."

Luke laughed and led Kennedy outside. A car slowed and pulled into the driveway. Luke jogged ahead to the compact car and opened the door. "Hop in."

As she slid into the car and exchanged pleasantries with the driver, Kennedy sighed and her heart rate slowed, allowing her to grow comfortable while chatting with Luke for the entire ride. By the time they reached the brewery, she dropped her shoulders and relaxed her neck. The dim lights, modern music, and glossy, live oak bar created a comfortable and familiar setting. "Ah. Much better." Kennedy grinned. "This is more my scene."

"And not an ugly Christmas sweater in sight." Luke selected a high-top table near the bar. He pulled out a chair for Kennedy and jogged to his spot across the table. He leaned in and tented his hands.

Kennedy tilted forward, as well. "So, Luke. What brought you to suburbia?" She hoped he didn't notice she was staring at his eyes, but she found looking anywhere else challenging.

"I don't have much of a story." He lowered his hands and drummed his fingers on the table. "Mine is the typical job opportunity tale. I'm a software consultant for a firm based out of London and bounced around the country from project to project for the past few years. The next step was moving to London permanently or traveling to assist another start-up guy out here. I have no desire to live abroad, never did, but I know these short-term gigs need to end. Living like a nomad is getting old." He chuckled and placed his hand to his chest. "Not that I'm getting any older, but you know. I told myself this would be the last stop and came here in October. When I was told 'near Muncie,' I envisioned a town a bit less rural, but so far, it's been great. I like Brian and want to see his idea take off, but as soon as it does, I'll need to find something else." Luke shrugged. "It's okay. I feel like it's time."

"So, living here is temporary?" Kennedy asked. *I hope I don't sound whiny. I should be relieved he's not a hometown boy. A transient might be a better fit. Then again, he sounds like he wants to pick a permanent place. Ugh, what am I getting into? I need to keep the conversation light and my eyes open.*

Luke nodded. "I'm staying in a corporate condo. A couple of weeks ago, Brian and I were talking about my living situation, and he immediately extended an invitation to tonight's party. I tried to decline, even fabricated travel plans, but Lexi called me directly and wouldn't take no for an answer."

"She's very convincing," Kennedy said.

"I'd use another word, but yours works, too."

Kennedy giggled. *I like his sense of humor. And his hands, and OMG what is happening? Light, remember!*

Their server hovered until a lull occurred in their laughter and introduced himself. "What can I get you this snowy evening?" He placed two coasters on the table. He turned to Kennedy.

Unfamiliar with the local beer, she ordered a house draft.

"Make that two and also a plate of your russet chips. Please."

The server nodded. "Absolutely. I'll be right back."

"Sound good? I kind of guessed, but I was here once before and thought they were great."

"Perfect." Kennedy grinned. "I'm more a salty than sweet kind of gal. I mean, for food. I was at a loss with the baking. You probably figured that out already."

"I'd like to figure out a lot more." Luke fiddled with the brown, cardboard coaster. "Your turn. Where are you from and all that?"

"My origin story. I'll need a beer." From the corner of her eye, Kennedy saw the server approaching with their pint glasses. "Just in time." She took a long sip and leaned back in her chair. "I'm a Cali girl. Grew up in southern, went to college in northern, and until a week ago, I lived and worked near San Francisco. I spent the last ten years at the same advertising agency."

The server reappeared and slid a basket onto the

table. "Your chips. Let me know if you need anything else."

Relieved to pause her story, Kennedy popped a potato chip into her mouth. The salt tasted like heaven

"California is a long way from Indiana." Luke reached for a chip. "Literally and metaphorically."

Nodding, she felt oddly comfortable sharing the truth. He seemed genuinely interested. "Well, I'm only here temporarily too. The house I'm living in was my aunt's. I still haven't called it my house yet, and I doubt I ever will. Aunt Maggie was my mother's aunt, so technically she was my great- or grand-aunt. I was close with her, and she visited us all the time, but believe it or not, this is the first time I've ever been here. She passed away a few months ago and left me the house." Kennedy's throat tightened, and she blinked rapidly to erase the sting of the threatening tears. Months had passed since she last relayed the information, but the pain still felt fresh.

"Wow, I'm sorry." Luke took a large gulp of his beer.

Kennedy smiled then raised a pointer finger and took a sip as well. The beer cooled her throat, enabling her to speak again. "Thank you. She generously bequeathed me the property, but she included specific instructions. Knowing I'd object to moving to small-town suburbia, she stipulated in her will that I have to live here for one year before I can sell."

"That's heavy." Luke raised his eyebrows.

"Yup. Aunt Maggie told my mother she expected me to fall in love with Poppy Lane and never want to leave."

"Aha." Luke smirked, and his eyes crinkled at the

edges. "What do you think?"

"It's perfectly fine for other people. Adults with families and stable careers, SUVs, and all that. I'll play by the rules, though, and stick it out. But…" She shook her head and took another sip. "This slow pace isn't for me."

Luke cocked his head. "A year is a long time. A lot could happen."

Heat crept up her neck. "We'll see."

"What about your job? What do you do at the advertising agency?"

"I'm a graphic artist, and I left the door open. Officially, I'm only taking a leave of absence, and I'm dabbling with freelance work. Truthfully, I'm not sure I want to return to the same advertising agency when I go back. I hope this adventure will help me decide."

Luke raised his glass. "Here's to seeing what's next."

Kennedy tapped her glass to his, making a *clink*. Relief washed over her, knowing the introduction portion of the evening passed. Normally, this was the awkward portion of a date, but Luke made it very easy and ended it on an encouraging note. Suddenly, her appetite returned, and she was glad for the salty chips and felt comfortable enough to dig in.

The next four hours passed quickly while they talked and watched college football games on the giant screens mounted above the bar. While he didn't support her team, she was relieved to discover a shared deep hatred for the school receiving all the media attention. The team was currently playing a big rival, and Kennedy enjoyed the mutual sentiment of hoping the team would lose.

During a bathroom break, Kennedy caught her beaming expression in the mirror. *Is it possible to be this happy with someone so quickly?* Part of her wanted to text her friends, "You'll never believe this," as she used to do in odd or exciting situations. But before removing her phone from her back pocket, she hesitated and refrained. Not wanting to share or jinx the wonderful evening, she turned off her phone. *Is this what living in the moment feels like?* Laughing at her reflection, she checked her teeth and smoothed her hair. As she reentered the bar, she caught sight of Luke, her heart skipping a beat.

He smiled and stood.

Resuming the previous relaxed conversations, Kennedy enjoyed losing track of time.

At ten, Luke ordered burgers and a third round of drinks.

At eleven, a group involved in a Christmas pub crawl swarmed the bar area. The boisterous bunch all wore Santa hats and broke into a round of holiday songs.

"I guess we can't escape the cheesy Christmas partygoers even here," Luke said.

"This town seems to take the holiday very seriously." Kennedy pointed to the decorations hanging from the ceiling. Ornaments dangled from the exposed pipes, and garland wound the support beams.

At midnight, their server dropped their bill on the table and dashed away without a word.

"Somebody wants to go home." Luke reached for his wallet.

Kennedy placed a hand over Luke's on the table. "Not me. I don't want to leave yet." The boldness surprised her, but she welcomed the surge of confidence.

Luke grinned. "Me neither. Let's settle here and have another at the bar."

"I need to stretch my legs anyway." Kennedy smirked and pushed back her chair.

Luke guided them through the standing-room-only crowd. He found an opening near the end of the bar and reached to bring Kennedy in and away from the servers' path. Luke kept his gaze fixed on her eyes as he reached for her hand.

Kennedy smiled and entwined her fingers with his. She had no choice but to lean into him to avoid the bustle of the crowd. "Sorry, tight quarters."

"I don't mind," Luke said.

A tightness filled her chest, but she didn't believe the sensation was due to nerves. Since meeting Luke, she felt relaxed. The ease allowed her to speak her mind, and maybe even her heart, with him.

Another beer was probably a bad idea, but Kennedy wanted a reason to stay longer. The prop would help. "And to think I almost bailed on the party."

"Me, too!"

"I have a feeling we would have ended up here together eventually. I do like the coincidence though. It adds a spark to the evening." Kennedy offered a small smile. She was aware to still be cautious.

Luke took an audible breath. "I have a confession. I told myself, if I didn't run into you at the store by next Wednesday, I'd call to ask you out for next weekend."

"No way." Kennedy fought to hide the smile she felt with her whole body. *He thought about me, too.*

"It gets worse. I also planned to grocery shop every

day. Now I can go back to ordering home-delivery online."

"Oh, you think you can, huh?" *Forget caution and keeping things light.*

Luke lowered his head. "Can I?"

Kennedy grinned. "Only if you tell me which service delivers to my block."

At last call, Luke suggested joining the rest of the crowd of thirtysomethings on the sidewalk. Every few seconds, a car bearing a rideshare sticker appeared.

From her back pocket, Kennedy retrieved and lifted her cell phone. "I got this, Luke. You have gone above and beyond all night. Hey, Scarlett, open the rideshare app."

"It's been my pleasure." Luke placed his hand on the small of her back as they waited for their car to arrive.

While in the bar, the snow had subsided, and a dusting coated the streets and sidewalks. Kennedy thought it made the town look fresh and festive. *Maybe Christmas will feel different this year.* When the car turned onto Poppy Lane, she was glad to see the lights twinkling on all the bushes. She wasn't glad to say goodbye to Luke. "Sorry to make you go out of your way by dropping me off first."

"I wouldn't have let you go alone," Luke said.

Though flattered he cared, she didn't want to seem weak. "I'd be fine. I've been alone all this time."

"Out of the question." Luke shook his head.

At her driveway, she turned. "Well…"

"Kennedy, I had such a better night than I could have ever imagined when I left my condo all those hours ago."

Despite the blush, she still felt confident. "Now that we're not going to grocery stores, when will I see you again?"

Luke snickered. "Tomorrow. I have to pick up my car." He pointed toward a snow-covered, silver sedan parked right in front of Aunt Maggie's house.

The coincidences just keep getting better. Kennedy grinned as she skipped up the steps. *Thank you, karma.*

Chapter Five

"Hey, Scarlett," Kennedy whispered. After several more attempts to prompt her phone, she stuck out her hand and blindly inched her fingers over the nightstand. A glass knocked over, making a *thunk.* Wincing, she prayed it was only water.

A pounding behind her temple amplified as Kennedy eased upright and squinted against the harsh sunlight streaming through the window. *How did I forget to pull the shade last night? Or was it this morning? When did I get to bed?* Scenes of entering the house rushed back. Kennedy remembered struggling to remove her tall boots, flopping on the couch, and furiously texting. *Who? Oh, no. Where is my phone? It must still be downstairs.* Rubbing her eyes, she spied the glass on its side, intact, and next to a tiny drop of water. A dab with the comforter soaked it up easily, but now she wished she had a full glass of water to combat the headache.

Pushing off the covers revealed only half of her pajamas. From the nightstand drawer, she selected a pair of flannel bottoms. The top was light blue, and the pants were red-and-green plaid. She shrugged and sauntered over to the mirror. "Ugh." She finger-combed her hair.

Descending the stairs was a challenge to her balance and socks. Kennedy slid a hand along the banister and headed toward the kitchen. Coffee was required, but her phone was a priority, so she turned into the living room.

"Hey, Scarlett?" Kennedy scanned the area. Her phone lay on the couch. Pressing the power button was pointless. The battery was completely drained. In the kitchen, she plugged her phone into a charger and brewed coffee. Half a cup and seven percent charge later, she tried her phone again.

"Good morning. Today is Sunday, December ninth, and the weather is sunny and thirty-one degrees Fahrenheit. You have nothing on your agenda."

"Thank God." Kennedy searched the cabinets for a bottle of pain reliever. "Hey, Scarlett, do I have any voicemails?"

"You have no new voicemails."

"Good." Kennedy lifted her phone and tapped the home screen. The text message icon indicated seventeen unread messages. "Not good." Nausea rose in Kennedy's throat. She gripped the mug. Years had passed since she last experienced a morning after of what-ifs. The dreaded sensation came crashing back. *Who did I text? What did I say? I wasn't that tipsy, but I was excited, and it was super late, so anything is possible. I just hope I didn't do anything to blow my chance with Luke.*

Kennedy gulped the rest of her coffee and placed the empty mug under the spout to brew another pod. While waiting, she hovered a forefinger over the messaging app to reveal who tried to reach her. Mom. Kennedy cringed.

—10 p.m. How was the cookie party?—

—11 p.m. Were the snowballs a hit?—

—12 a.m. I guess you are having fun—

—12:12 a.m. Goodnight—

Ugh. Ellen would have to wait. More coffee was necessary to determine what to share, so she sipped and checked the other messages.

Kennedy discovered she texted her friends in California and told them about her night and previous encounters with Luke. Gritting her teeth, she scrolled through the conversations and was relieved to discover she hadn't gushed or revealed too much. They exchanged remarks for about forty-five minutes, then Kennedy must have gone to bed. The friends in the earlier time zone continued to ask questions without getting a response. They gave up at three a.m.

The last text was from Luke. Her stomach flipped. Thankfully, it was the only text exchange besides the emojis they swapped in the store on Friday. Relief washed over her, and she tapped on the message he sent an hour ago.

—My next-door neighbor is dropping me off to pick up my car at 10:30. He offered and only time he could go. Couldn't refuse. Grab brunch? No worries if not. Last minute, I know.—

Ten thirty? That is, like now! Kennedy liked the text and sent a separate smile emoji. She ran up the stairs in search of a less clashing outfit. While brushing her teeth, she mentally rehearsed an explanation for Ellen. Kennedy hoped the mint would do the trick for her breath, then haphazardly sprayed a cloud of daisy-scented body mist while she tugged on black, ripped jeans and a fluffy, pink sweatshirt. She opened Ellen's contact, but the startling sound of the doorbell interrupted her apology.

Kennedy shoved her phone into the kangaroo pouch of her sweatshirt and smoothed her hair one last time before opening the door. "Luke." Kennedy smiled and swept her arm inside. "I overslept and just got your text. I'm sorry. I need a second to find a hair elastic." He looked too awake for a morning after a night out, but she was relieved to see he wore running pants and a hoodie under his usual peacoat.

"No worries. Please take your time." He stepped inside and pulled off his gray gloves. "I would never have come by this early, but my sweet, elderly neighbor called to invite me to church. While explaining I had to pick up my car, he offered to drop me on his way. I had to promise I'd go with him next week." Luke blushed.

Kennedy tilted her head and smiled. She mentally chalked another point for Luke. Maggie would approve of a churchgoer. "I kinda need to attend, too. I'm sure my aunt's church friends noticed my absence. But today—brunch is necessary. I'll be right back." She pointed to her hair and rolled her eyes.

"Looks fine to me, but you do whatever you need. I'm in no rush."

"Thanks. Make yourself at home. Please note the furniture was inherited as well. The fabric and pattern choices were not mine. I like cabbage roses, but not on sofas."

Luke laughed and sunk into a wing chair.

Ten minutes later, Kennedy descended the stairs. Her hair was arranged in a high bun, and last night's eyeliner had been removed and reapplied with a faint line to give the illusion of being fully awake. She passed on other makeup. Luke seemed to be very down-to-earth, and she didn't feel the need to cover up anything or add to impress. A calm replaced the nerves from earlier, and she practically floated into the living room. "Okay. I'm as ready as I'll ever be this morning." Kennedy stopped in her tracks.

Luke was not alone.

"Good morning." Lexi stood in the middle of the living room, holding three matching clear, plastic containers topped with blue lids.

Luke's eyes widened. "I was explaining to Lexi that we have her to thank for meeting at the party last night."

"Looks like you did more than just meet." Lexi winked.

Kennedy sliced both hands through the air as if to erase the last statement. "No, um, Luke didn't stay over. He's here to get his car." She pointed toward the window. "We took a rideshare last night. After the party, that is. Your awesome party. Really great party."

"Oh, please. You're adults, and you don't need to explain anything. I'm tickled to hear I'm responsible. Maybe it was my special drink." She cocked her head and grinned. "Anyway, I won't hold you up. I only came to drop off your six dozen." After she handed the boxes to Kennedy, Lexi turned to Luke. "If I'd known you'd be here, I would've grabbed yours, too. I think Brian plans to bring them to work tomorrow." Lexi pivoted on her heels and walked out of the room but hesitated by the door.

"Thanks," Luke shouted through the hall in her wake.

Oh my gosh. Where are my manners? Kennedy snapped to attention and caught up to her neighbor. "Wait, Lexi, let me see you out. Thanks again, for everything."

"You betcha. And—way to go!" Waggling her fingers, she turned and left.

Kennedy walked back to the living room, shaking her head. "Awkward."

"Totally," Luke said. "But funny."

Depositing the containers on the kitchen table, she gasped. "Oh my God. Boxes. That's what Lexi meant on the invitation."

"What?" Luke asked.

She shook her head. "Never mind. I'm already so embarrassed. Let's go eat."

Luke slowly navigated the side streets of Meadow Ridge, which boasted a speed limit of fifteen while Kennedy used her phone to search brunch options. After several attempts to locate a decent restaurant for mimosas and custom omelets, she announced brunch could only be found downtown and by reservation. "Oh, no." Kennedy's voice wavered. "I was really looking forward to it." She slumped her shoulders.

"Don't worry. We'll do brunch another time." Luke patted her hand. "I think there's a diner on Main Street. Wanna check it out?"

Her mood lifted. "Sounds good. A greasy, alcohol-free breakfast is probably what I need this morning anyway." Kennedy's stomach grumbled loudly, overshadowing the butterflies she felt after hearing he wanted to make future plans. Placing a hand over her midsection, she giggled.

"Not a moment too soon." Luke laughed and swung his car into a parking spot in front of Don and Judi's Diner. The glass front displayed spray-painted snowflakes and singing angels.

Inside, a hostess motioned to a back booth. Next to the booth sat a family of six all wearing snowman costumes.

Trying not to laugh or make a loud comment, Kennedy slid into the booth and out of her bulky jacket.

Over scrambled eggs and hash browns, Luke told Kennedy more about his job and how he chose his career path.

She shared her frustration with working for a large firm, and her freelance plans. Kennedy enjoyed discussing work and bosses with Luke, but she felt distracted by her attraction. Despite her best attempts, she couldn't stop staring at Luke's eyes. "Blue."

"What?" Luke asked.

She squinted. "Your eyes. I thought they were green, but today they look blue."

Luke chuckled. "Yeah, they do that. They change depending on what I wear. This blue hoodie makes them appear blue. Truly, I don't know what color they are."

"Well, today they are blue, and I think your chameleon thing is very cool." *And hot.*

Commotion stirred as the family of snowmen prepared to leave. Pulling on mittens and affixing top hats, they shuffled their way between tables. The mom turned briefly, made eye contact with Kennedy, and offered a wide smile.

The server reappeared with a raised glass coffeepot. "One more cup?"

"Yes," Kennedy replied.

"Me, too." Luke thanked the server and turned to Kennedy. "I don't need any more caffeine, but I don't want to go yet."

Recalling the same sentiment about last night's final beer, heat rose to Kennedy's cheeks. "I'm having a good time, too." She cleared her throat. "So, what are your Sunday rituals?"

"Laundry and watch football. I usually call my parents and video chat with my brothers about our fantasy league. Dorky, I know." He tilted his head. "How about you?"

"I'm not sure. I've only been here a short time, and I'm still not used to the fact that I don't go into an office tomorrow. I have no need to iron." Kennedy lifted both hands. "Actually, I watch all the NFL games, too, and I'll probably clean the house."

"Your house, you mean?" Luke raised an eyebrow.

Kennedy shook her head. "I haven't gotten used to that either."

"So, you won't be naming your house like you did your phone?" Luke blew on his coffee and sipped.

"Funny. But no. I doubt I'll ever call it mine. I feel like I'm staying in someone else's space. Like I'm playing grown-up in a dollhouse. Am I making any sense?"

He nodded. "I get it. I never feel quite settled in either, but the difference is I look forward to having the sensation. I hope to find a sense of belonging soon." Luke stacked a neat pile of cash on the table and slid out of the booth.

"I don't think I'll feel that way about Meadow Ridge." Kennedy zipped her coat and stood to meet Luke.

During the car ride back, radio announcers made game-day predictions.

With a huff, she pointed toward the radio. "The

point spread on the noon game is totally inflated. These announcers are biased. I think three points is more than generous."

At a red traffic light, Luke turned toward Kennedy. "Wow. You know your stuff. Do you prefer statistics or particular players or teams?"

"I love all aspects of the game." She circled her arms. "Go ahead. Ask me anything."

"Hmm." Luke bunched his eyebrows and proceeded through an intersection. "Okay. What do you think of my fantasy team lineup?" He listed a dozen names and grinned.

Nodding with recognition after each name, she mentally calculated. She hesitated only a moment to purse her lips while considering her response. "Not bad. I worry about your punter, though. He's inconsistent at best."

As Luke pulled his car into the driveway, he laughed. "Here you are—the house."

The words stung Kennedy, and she suddenly wished to bring back the fun banter from before the discussion about her living situation. She also didn't want to say goodbye yet. "You want to come in for a bit?"

"I'd love to, but I have to confess my phone is blowing up about the first game. I guess it already started. I lost track of time." From the pocket of his hoodie, Luke lifted his phone. The screen was filled with notification bubbles. "Also, I have no clean socks and have to go into Brian's office by eight. Tomorrow will be a big day. We're meeting with the investors. So, socks are necessary, and I should also prep for the presentation." He repocketed the phone and ran his hands through his hair. "Can I walk you to the door?"

Lowering her gaze, she nodded.

On the front step, Luke took both of Kennedy's hands and inhaled. "Will the neighbors notice if I kiss you?"

Kennedy smirked. "Absolutely. Let's give them something to talk about." She hoped to sound confident, but her knees weakened. She shifted her weight and leaned toward Luke.

Luke met her halfway and touched her cheek before kissing her.

His touch was gentle, and the kiss was soft and sweet, the way Kennedy thought a first kiss should be. The warm feeling left her wishing it would last longer and made her hope for more in the future. She pulled back and wrapped her arms around Luke's neck for an embrace. Her cheeks stretched tightly around her wide smile.

Luke kept one arm around Kennedy's waist and glanced around the neighborhood. "Ask Scarlett if I can call you later."

"I'm sure she will remind me to call you if you don't." Inside, she stared at the striped wallpaper and replayed the kiss and conversations. Several minutes passed before she snapped back to reality and remembered to call her mom. After an hour on the phone with Ellen apologizing for ignoring her calls and texts, Kennedy finally showered and powered on the TV. Her favorite team had a substantial lead, so while watching, she replied to the last of her friends' texts and successfully evaded revealing her true feelings. She admitted to having fun and told them he was cute, but she did not confess to being totally smitten. The sky was dark by the time she remembered the moving boxes. “Hey, Scarlett,” she called out. “Set a reminder to go through the boxes tomorrow.”

“Okay,” the digital voice answered.

After heating a can of soup and toasting a roll for dinner, Kennedy snuggled into the couch and felt content, but not completely relaxed. Something was missing. Maybe it was a lack of a routine? Maybe homesickness? She talked to her mom and friends and her team was winning, so what was the void? While considering a Christmas cookie to cheer her, a buzz emitted from the couch cushion beside her. She spied her screen.

—New York sucks.—

While laughing out loud, she responded to Luke’s text.

—Not as bad as Cleveland.—

—True. Whatcha doing?—

—Eating soup and watching my team win. You?—

—Ouch. Soup?! I’m matching my socks. Maybe we do belong in suburbia.—

—Lol. I peeked at the cookies, and I have a long way to go to fit in around here.—

Kennedy rose and walked to the kitchen. She snapped a photo of a delicate, jelly-filled sugar cookie in the perfect shape of a snowflake and sent the image to Luke.

—No way someone on your block made that.—

—Agree. But that would be against the rules.—

—No doubt!—

—Uh-oh, Mom calling again.—

—No worries. Call you after work tomorrow?—

—Yes, please—

She added a smile emoji then set aside her phone. Kennedy spent most of Monday at her laptop. Since relocating upstairs, she found concentrating on her work easier. The boxes, however, remained pushed against the walls of the living room and mudroom. Kennedy launched her blog, and the website now sported a banner announcing *Coming Soon*.

For breakfast, she ate three gingerbread men, and lunch was the remnants of a leftover, soggy salad. A week had passed since she last grocery shopped, and she had yet to join a home delivery service. Dinner would have to be more cookies or take-out. At six, she dialed the closest Thai restaurant. Once the craving for *Lard Nar* hit, nothing else would do, even after discovering delivery wasn't available in her neighborhood.

Scarlett recited the directions to a parking spot at a small strip mall. Kennedy expected a real restaurant, not the takeout counter this appeared to offer. *Oh, boy, this better be good.* She turned back to remotely lock her door and had to shield her eyes with her purse to block the blinding headlights of an approaching car. A silver sedan parked directly next to her. The car looked familiar.

Luke emerged and immediately burst out laughing. "What are the chances?"

"A snowball's?" Kennedy couldn't hide her wide grin. *The coincidences never cease. I hope they never do!*

"Exactly." Still laughing, Luke opened the restaurant door and waved a hand inside. "After you. This is too funny. I planned to call you while I enjoyed strip mall *Pad Thai* from my couch. But how about you join me? We can even sit at the table."

Though she tried not to smirk, Kennedy couldn't think of anything she'd rather do. With her brown, paper takeout bag on the passenger seat and the aroma of garlic sauce consuming her car, Kennedy followed Luke's sedan for a mile to his condo complex. Despite the overwhelming scent of her dinner, the thought of more time with him made her forget all about eating.

Fumbling with his keys, Luke unlocked the door to a small, but modern, space. "Oops!" He rushed inside and scooped papers, pens, cups, and a laptop from the dining table. "Sorry, I guess I use it more as a desk than anything."

"No apologies. I only recently relocated from the kitchen table to a sewing room." Kennedy arranged the dinners and sat. As always with Luke, she felt at ease and comfortable talking about any subject. "So, did your parents recently relocate to Florida?"

Luke deposited forks and napkins beside the containers. "I was a junior at Ohio State when my parents decided to sell everything and move to Miami. I was rendered homeless. I sorta have been ever since with all the moving around." He shrugged.

"Wow. At least I was living on my own when mine sold and moved to Naples two years ago." Kennedy removed the lid to her dinner, and steam rose to her face. Undeterred, she scooped a forkful.

"I'm flying down on the twenty-second. What about you?" Luke speared a tofu triangle.

Picking up her napkin, Kennedy covered her mouth to prevent the garlic-laden noodles from slipping out mid-laugh. "The next day."

Luke joined in her giggles and reached for her

hand. "Too bad Florida is such a big state."

Flattered, but not knowing how to respond, Kennedy nodded and made a joke about Christmas in the south. She felt as interested in him as he sounded about her but was unsure how much to reveal so soon. Joking was a comfortable diversion—for now.

Luke relayed tales of growing up in Cleveland and working in Dallas, Manhattan, and Chicago. An hour later, Luke rose. "I'll clear. Go make yourself comfortable on the couch. I'll be right there." He turned toward the kitchen, then swiveled his head. "Oh, and same as you, none of the furniture is mine. It all came with the rental, so no judging. I'd have picked a soft, brown leather, not this tough, black stuff."

"No worries," Kennedy called from the next room.

A few minutes later, Luke returned and settled next to Kennedy, and the couch squeaked.

"Nice," she said. "Yeah, sometimes I imagine how I'd redecorate, and then I remember I'm not staying."

He frowned. "You really miss California, don't you?"

Did he seem disappointed? Kennedy cocked her head and was silent for a moment. She wanted to be honest but not sound stubborn. She took a deep breath. "Good question. I don't know if it's the location I miss so much as the familiarity."

Luke nodded. "I haven't had that in so long I forgot the feeling. Funny, though, living here, I'm actually closer to home than I've ever been. My brothers are in Ohio—practically next door." He twisted his lips. "Actually, it's like a six-hour drive."

"That's still closer than I am to home or my family. I'm not sure how I really feel about Meadow Ridge.

This is all new to me," Kennedy said in a soft voice.

"New can be good." Luke reached an arm around Kennedy's shoulders.

She snuggled in closer and detected a minty scent. Had he secretly brushed his teeth? If so, she admired the effort. "True." *And so far, so good.*

"Can you stay for a movie?" he asked.

"How about the Monday night game?"

Luke grinned and grabbed the TV remote. "Even better."

After the first quarter, Luke rose. "I'll be right back."

She wrinkled her brows. *Whoa. I'm a goner. Talk about unfamiliar feelings...I can't remember the last time I anxiously awaited a guy's appearance. Maybe not since high school.* She straightened her posture, tucked her legs under her butt, and silently reminded herself not to appear lovestruck.

Luke returned holding a plate piled with Christmas cookies. "Dessert?"

Kennedy laughed and selected a snowman-shaped, frosted sugar cookie.

"Sorry, there were no salt cookies."

"I believe they're called pretzels." Grinning, she bit off the snowman's top hat. While not usually a sweet fan, she welcomed the sugary icing as it erased the lingering garlic.

Luke tossed a thumbprint cookie into his mouth and placed the plate on the coffee table. He finished chewing and sunk back into the couch. "Brian couldn't wait to deliver these today. He asked if I enjoyed the party and winked."

"So cheesy." *Seriously, are the Gen Xers and*

Boomers on my block so desperate for gossip that they care about my life? Pathetic.

"I know. But, in a sincere effort to quell your block's gossip, I told him we already knew each other through a mutual acquaintance."

"Liar." Kennedy punched his arm.

"No lie. I met Scarlett first, and you two go way back." He shrugged. "I was only defending your honor." A smirk spread across his face.

Unsure if he was being serious, Kennedy was at a loss for a good comeback. Wanting to lighten the mood she leaned in and gave him a quick kiss. "Thank you."

Luke smirked and cupped her cheek. "Anytime. My turn."

Kennedy suddenly felt like Florida would feel much too large.

****

On Friday night, Kennedy braced herself for a long conversation. "Hey, Scarlett, call Mom."

"Kennedy! I haven't heard from you all week. How are you?"

Taking a deep breath, she prepared her summary. Normally, she never went this long without calling, and guilt set in. "I'm great, Mom. I've been really busy. Let's see. I've made a lot of progress with my website. Snow fell all day today, and the neighbor boy, Caleb, is shoveling right now. I was supposed to meet up with Luke—you know the guy I met at the grocery store? Anyway, the office he works for threw an impromptu holiday party in the conference room where he is working temporarily, and now he's stuck. We're going to some town event tomorrow that the neighbors insist I attend. Apparently, Aunt Maggie was always a big part of the preparations."

"*Chriskindlemart*."

"What the what?"

"It's like a German Christmas bazaar with little shops and booths. Your generation would call it a pop-up."

"Oh," Kennedy muttered as she searched the foreign word on her tablet.

"You'll have a great time. I can't wait to hear all about it and this Luke. Yay, only one week until you're here!"

"Yeah, one week. Yay." She feigned excitement for her mother's benefit, but Kennedy's heart sank. In one week, she'd be away from Luke. In the past week, she'd only been apart from him for one night. *I'm in deep, and Mom will know from taking one look at me. I already miss him, and I haven't even left yet.*

Chapter Six

Standing before the full-length, bedroom mirror, Kennedy buttoned her new, ivory wool coat and smiled at her reflection. Unlike the short, puffy coat from her friends, this more dressed-up version fell to her knees. Kennedy saw enough Christmas movies to determine she needed a long coat. She spun and nodded. *Maybe I can embrace winter weather.* She stuffed the suede mittens her mother sent into the pockets and picked up a black-and-white, knit hat. The faux mink pom-pom on its top was irresistible.

Her phone buzzed.

Rushing to the window, she peered out and spied the now-familiar, silver car. After practically skipping down the steps like a giddy child, she flew outside in a flash.

Luke opened the passenger door and jogged to the driver's side.

When Kennedy slid onto the worn leather, she sighed. The car was toasty, and the seat warmer was already on.

Luke reappeared and reached into the backseat. "I got you a gift."

"Aw. You didn't have to do that."

"I couldn't resist." Luke pointed to the gray beanie on his head. "I was ordering myself this sweet hat and thought of you when I spotted the scarf on the site."

Luke held a furry, shell-pink infinity scarf.

"It's perfect." Kennedy wound it around her neck. Leaning over the console to give Luke a quick peck on the cheek to thank him, she instead kissed him with a fierceness that surprised her. She pulled back and was pleased to see Luke's eyes were as wide as saucers.

"Wow." He blinked several times. "If that's your reaction to gifts, then let's go shopping."

"Ha. Maybe that's my reaction to you. Anyway, let's go to this *Chriskindlemart* thing. Lexi stopped by this morning to make sure I was still going. Apparently, she has something to show me." Kennedy fastened her seatbelt.

Luke raised his eyebrows and shifted into Drive. After talking and driving a few blocks, he turned up the volume on the car's radio. A familiar Christmas song played. "This okay? The station switched from contemporary to twenty-four-hour Christmas music last week. I could change it or stream from my phone."

"Leave it. The music will help us prepare for that." Kennedy pointed out the windshield. In front of the town hall stood an enormous, hand-painted sign welcoming them to the *North Pole*.

The town square was blocked off by construction horses adorned with garland and wreaths. Christmas music played over speakers hanging from streetlamps. Wooden stalls painted red and white dotted the street. Some featured awnings with scalloped edging, others resembled small cottages.

Mr. and Mrs. Claus strolled through the crowds. Kids dressed as elves skipped behind the couple and handed out candy canes.

Luke parked on a side street and opened the door

for Kennedy. "Where to first?"

Kennedy scanned the area and pointed toward a stall featuring hot cider and mulled wine. "Let's start there and make our way around with something warm to drink."

Gripping souvenir mugs, Kennedy and Luke navigated through kids carrying hot chocolate and bags of popcorn. The stalls offered numerous Christmas ornaments, local crafts, homemade fudge, and peppermint bark.

Luke held Kennedy's mittened hand and slowed as they approached the last two booths.

"There you are."

Upon hearing the familiar voice of her neighbor, Kennedy paused before the second-to-last booth.

"Having fun?" A sign proclaiming *Meadow Ridge Real Estate Agency* hung above Lexi's head.

Aha. The canvas sign was big, bold, and blah, but Kennedy smiled. "This is great! Looks like the whole town is here," she said with a cheery tone.

"Pretty much. This is always a very popular event. Second only to the Fourth of July parade and concert. Some years we freeze, but this weather is perfect for a good turnout." Lexi leaned across the top of the booth and cupped her hands around her mouth. "It's also a great opportunity to advertise if you know what I mean. That's what I wanted to talk to you about."

"Oh." Kennedy fiddled with her new scarf.

"If you're interested, I might have an opportunity. I heard you're doing freelance graphic design now."

Kennedy side-eyed Luke.

"I might have mentioned something." Luke shrugged.

"Yeah, I'm just getting started, but I'd be happy to draft some ideas."

Lexi clapped. "Perfect." She slid a business card across the booth's surface. "Check out the website listed here, and you can use this address to email me. I can't wait to see what you come up with. Now, make sure you visit next door." Lexi tilted her head toward the last stall.

Following directions, Kennedy took two steps to her right and leaned in to view the wares. Cookies of all shapes and sizes adorned plates featuring tented name placards.

Lorna's Lemon Squares–Lorna Franklin

Ginny's Gingersnaps–Ginny Hamilton

Stained Glass Cookies by the Church League

Snowballs in Memory of Maggie

Kennedy finished reading all ten placards and glanced at Luke.

Raising his eyebrows, Luke pointed at a plate of perfectly round, equally sized, powdered sugar balls.

"So that's what they were supposed to look like." Kennedy shook her head. "I wasn't even close."

"Wasn't your aunt's name Maggie?"

"Yes, this has to be about her, don't you think?" She pressed a hand to her chest.

"There's a chance…" Luke said.

Laughing, she hip-bumped him.

Luke regained his balance and pulled her close to his side.

An older woman wearing a frilly, eyelet apron approached the laughing couple. "Could I interest you in some cookies? They're the best."

Kennedy tilted her head and smiled. "Thank you,

but I have more than I'll ever need at home. We went to a cookie exchange party last weekend."

"Isn't that nice," the woman replied.

Blushing, Kennedy wondered if Luke noticed her use of the word "we" and hoped she didn't seem presumptuous. While she felt like they were a couple, she had only known him for a short time and had yet to define the relationship. "Yes, it was great." Suddenly choked up, she cleared her throat. "I do have a question about one of the plates here, though. My name is Kennedy Moore, and my aunt was Maggie Stanton. I was wondering if the snowballs here are in her memory."

The woman laced her fingers over her middle, and her face lit up. "Why, of course, they are, dear. Maggie was famous for her snowball cookies."

Kennedy nodded. "That explains a lot."

"Honey, I'm so happy to see you here. Maggie talked so much about you while you were growing up. I feel like I know you." The woman smiled and pointed toward the display. "The church gals did their best to replicate her recipe. We all miss her."

"That's such a sweet gesture. She would be touched. I certainly am." Knowing she met one of Maggie's friends, Kennedy felt an instant sense of peace.

"And I'm sure Mags would be thrilled to know you're settling in here." The woman touched Kennedy's arm and turned to help a little boy locate a chocolate chip cookie.

Kennedy resisted the urge to ask Scarlett to set a church reminder. She linked her arm through Luke's and wandered around the square, returning the numerous wishes of Merry Christmas offered. She asked to stop at a few of the booths she noticed earlier, and Kennedy bought a snow globe featuring the town square for her mom. She was having a great time, but she was getting colder and didn't want Luke to notice her shivering. She didn't want to seem weak or like a complainer, but mostly she didn't want the date to end if she admitted to being cold.

"Brrr." Luke pulled his hat over his ears. "I see an empty picnic table over by a fire pit." Removing a bare hand from his jacket pocket, he pointed to a group of tables dotting the middle of the square.

Kennedy spied several small, but blazing, fires. They filled the air with a comforting, smoky scent.

"Why don't you go grab it? I saw something I need, but I'll be right back." Luke shoved his hand back into his pocket.

Glad he also wanted to get warm, Kennedy hurried to the table and scooted as close to the fire as possible. She extended her feet to better feel the heat.

A moment later, Luke returned carrying a giant pretzel on a white paper plate. Steam rose to his face. "Care to share a salt cookie?"

"Absolutely." Kennedy pulled off a chunk of the hot dough. The salty treat warmed her all over. The muscles in her face relaxed.

After a few minutes, Lexi's husband, Brian, appeared.

"Hope you don't mind me warming for a minute. I've been out here setting up since early this morning." He held his hands near the fire.

"Good to see you outside of the office," Luke said.

"Same." Brian turned toward Kennedy. "I'm glad

you got him away from the computer today, Kennedy. He'd been working around the clock until you moved in." He elbow-nudged Luke. "Seriously though, Luke is a welcome asset. In the short time he's been here, he's become essential. I don't know how I could go live with the new platform without his guidance."

"Brian gives me too much credit." Luke waved a hand. "His new algorithm will be a great success. Just wait until after the first of the year, and you'll see software companies lining up to purchase the package."

"Well, if that's true, I might need you to stay here and oversee the distribution." Brian clapped Luke's back and turned again to face Kennedy. "Let's see if we can convince this nomad to put down some roots like you, Kennedy."

Tightness in her throat prevented her from responding. *Does everyone on my block assume I'm here for good and looking to settle down? I didn't feel like getting into details at the party, but maybe I should have informed Lexi. At least Luke knows the truth.* Brian's phone buzzed, and she was grateful.

"The boss is texting. Lexi needs me to bring the car around to pack her stuff." Brian waved goodbye and disappeared back into the crowd.

Silence followed in Brian's wake, and Kennedy picked at the last of the pretzel which had hardened and gone cold. "I guess I never told Lexi I'm only here temporarily."

Luke cleared his throat. "I have been thinking about it."

"About what?" Kennedy opened her fist and released the last chunk of pretzel onto the paper plate.

"Staying. You know, putting down roots or settling

down. Whatever it's called." Luke fidgeted with his gloves.

A flutter bubbled in Kennedy's stomach. She widened her eyes. "Adulting. Yikes."

Luke grinned. "Yeah, um, never mind. We can talk another time. This is kind of heavy for an afternoon date."

"True." Relieved to be done with subject, Kennedy smiled. "I think we're supposed to be enjoying the moment and feeling all sorts of Christmas cheer."

"Hmm." Luke stood. "I guess now is a good time for this. Kennedy, do you trust me?"

"Oh, boy." Kennedy rolled her eyes but was intrigued. "Sure. Why not?"

Grasping both her hands, Luke pulled Kennedy to her feet. "Follow me." He released a hand and motioned toward the giant hardware store.

"We're going in here?" She pointed.

Luke turned his head and flashed a tight smile. "Nope." He picked up his pace and disappeared around the back of the store.

Though puzzled and intrigued by his devilish grin, she followed him to the parking lot. Or, what used to be the parking lot. Dozens of Christmas trees now covered the asphalt. The scent of evergreen and pine overwhelmed the crisp, afternoon air. Kennedy found Luke standing beside a six-foot balsam fir. The branches were full and the fragrance strong.

He pointed then blew on his hands. "How about this one?"

"It's beautiful. But isn't it kind of big for your condo?"

"Of course, it's too big, but the tree is not for me.

No one would see it. The tree is for your living room." He stretched his arms and formed a frame with his hands. "I picture it right in front of the bay window."

Wow. He gave this a lot of thought. I'm touched and a little embarrassed I dismissed the idea. I should be more open to embracing Christmas. As she searched for the right response, Kennedy cocked her head and scrunched her face.

"Haven't you noticed everyone else on your block has a Christmas tree in their front window?"

"I noticed. I hoped nobody else would. I thought I could get away without one, but the little girl next door asked why my dad hasn't put up my tree yet." She winced.

"Ouch," Luke said. "That settles it. I'll call the guy to strap it to the roof of my car."

"But I don't have any ornaments or garland or whatever." Kennedy raised both hands.

"What about that box marked *Christmas Decorations-Tree Skirt* in your mudroom?"

"I don't know what you're talking about. At least three or four boxes are stacked in there. I haven't exactly categorized."

His grin returned. "I bumped into one the other day when I was hanging my jacket, and I noticed the label. I turned the box in hopes you wouldn't see it. I thought you'd back out if you knew I devised this evil plan." Luke rubbed his hands.

Kennedy punched his shoulder.

"Did it work? I want this to be my Christmas gift to you."

Kennedy threw her arms around his neck and hugged him. "Only if you promise to help me decorate and stay for dinner."

"Deal." He kissed her cheek. "Let's go. I'm freezing."

After Luke struggled to remove the tree from the top of his small sedan, he needed assistance.

Kennedy rushed to the basement for the metal stand and returned to help shove the monstrosity into the house.

The tree scraped the ceiling only once. After the minor struggle, the balsam stood majestically before the large bay window.

Arm in arm, Kennedy and Luke stood facing the tree.

"It's lights first, then ornaments." Luke held a strand of white lights.

"No." Kennedy shook a handful of garland. "I think it's garland, ornaments, then lights last."

"Aww." Luke leaned into Kennedy. "Our first fight."

"Ugh." She gave a playful push and removed her phone from the back pocket of her jeans. "Hey, Scarlett, what is the order of decorating a Christmas tree?"

"From the website All Things Christmas, the most efficient manner to decorate a tree is to first string lights, then hang ornaments and tinsel or garland. Finally, add a traditional angel or star at the very top."

Kennedy frowned.

Luke shuffled in a victory dance.

He's cute when he wins. I must look like a sore loser—not a cute look. I'll summon a smile, but not before I explain. "In my defense, though, my parents always had an artificial tree, and the lights never came off. The small version I had at my apartment was pre-lit *and* pre-decorated." Kennedy threw up her arms. "Anyway, I concede. Hey, Scarlett, find the best-rated Italian restaurant that delivers to this location. Please display the menu." She turned to Luke and offered her phone. "This will be a long night. Pick out a couple of entrees and a salad. I'll go open some wine."

Later, Kennedy swept the last of the fallen needles into a dustpan.

Luke hummed as he carried the empty decoration boxes to the garage. "Ready to kick up your feet and enjoy our creation?" He returned to the family room.

"Absolutely!" Kennedy settled onto the couch. "I'm already there. Come join me." She patted the cushion beside her and poured the last of the Merlot into stemless glasses.

Luke lowered onto the floral antique and scooted closer. He rested his head on her shoulder.

Kennedy passed him a glass and raised her own. "To a job well done."

They toasted and sipped until their glasses were empty.

Taking both glasses and placing them on the side table, Luke then leaned in for a kiss.

Heat rose on her neck. Not wanting the kiss to end, she gripped his upper arm and pulled in tighter. He smelled like the tree. *Like how Christmas is supposed to smell.*

As Luke ran his hands through her hair, he deepened the kiss. Shifting his legs, ankles became entwined.

This is amazing. I could stay in his arms all night. I can even hear angels singing. Oh, no. That's real singing and it sounds close. Kennedy pulled away and pouted. “Do you hear that?”

“No.” Luke kissed her neck.

“Yeah,” Kennedy whispered. “Me neither.”

Cupping her chin, Luke resumed the kiss.

The singing grew louder.

Her eyes flew open. Through the bay window, she spied a crowd gathered on her lawn. “Luke.” Kennedy tapped Luke’s shoulder. “We’re being watched.”

Straightening, Luke swiveled to look out the window. “Carolers.”

“What do we do?”

Luke’s shoulders dropped. He extracted his ankle. “I think we’re supposed to open the door to listen and thank them. At least, that’s what they do in Christmas movies.”

“Can’t we just hide?” Kennedy ran a hand over Luke’s chest.

“We’re already busted.” Luke rose. “C’mon. This is part of embracing Christmas and giving Poppy Lane a shot.”

“Fine. But only for a minute.” Kennedy lifted a hand to allow Luke to pull her.

From the doorway, Kennedy listened to two more songs. She grinned and tapped a foot but counted the seconds before she could return to Luke’s embrace.

Luke hummed and clapped, but between songs, he offered Kennedy a wink.

The crowd consisted of adults and children of all ages and singing abilities. They asked Kennedy and Luke to join in the last, which was a familiar kids’ tune. A few neighbors raised their eyebrows, but most simply smiled or waved at the couple before traveling to the next house.

"Okay," Luke said. "Where were we?"

A smile of relief stretched Kennedy's cheeks upon hearing he'd had his fill of neighborhood friendliness but not enough of her.

****

"Hey, Scarlett. Call Mom." Kennedy adjusted the stiff, floral sofa pillow wedged behind her back.

"How was your weekend, honey?"

For the last hour, Kennedy struggled with telling her mom about the tree and keeping the special night to herself. Closing her eyes, she replayed the fun and the intimate moments she had shared with Luke. *I don't want to break the spell. Being with him feels like a dream I don't want to share.*

"Kennedy? You still there?"

"Yeah." She shook her head and took a sip from the reusable water bottle in her tight grip. "Sorry, I uh, dropped the phone."

"You've been doing that a lot lately. Anyway, your dad and I are so excited to see you on Saturday! We shopped all weekend. Well, we played some pickleball with the Petersons too, but I got all my shopping done, and this week I'll get your favorites from the grocery store. Speaking of the grocery store, have you had any more dates with the guy you met by the butter?"

Decision time. She aimed the remote at the TV and muted the football game. "So, yeah, Luke." Kennedy sat straighter, took a deep breath, and exhaled. "I know I told you it was not a big deal, but that was before I knew him well, and okay, I wasn't ready for one of your inquisitions. But recently, things have changed. We've become close. We spent a lot of time together this past week, and I guess you'd say we're moving fast, but I don't know—it feels right." Kennedy let out a breath and bit her lip. She hoped this was enough information to satisfy her mother and prevent further digging.

"Oh, honey! I'm so happy for you. Just be careful about moving fast, but I guess that's not too surprising at your age. You're old enough to know what you're doing. I know you don't think so, but news flash—you're an adult."

Wow. Am I really getting off so easily? I'd better quit while I'm ahead. "Thanks, Mom. I promise to be cautious. You don't need to worry."

When the subject abruptly changed to the reality show they both watched, Kennedy sunk back into the couch with a sigh of relief. *Hopefully this will hold Ellen until she sees the sappy looks on my face next week.*

Chapter Seven

Ping.

—Landed—

Pushing back from her desk, Kennedy removed her earbuds and paused the video she was creating for Lexi's real estate agency website. Tweaking the close-ups was challenging. A break was necessary. She raised her phone and read Luke's text for the fifth time. *Well, he is officially there.* The distance felt tangible. She swiveled and rose from the chair, then walked toward the window facing the backyard. A cardinal trilled, and she spied it perched on an evergreen branch. She tapped the screen.

—Good luck with your grandmother!—

Only yesterday, Luke discovered Gram would also be spending Christmas at the Miami house on the golf course.

—Thx. Waiting for my clubs to arrive in the oversized area. Gram wants to play 9 before dinner. Dinner probs at 4:30 so should be interesting.—

Absently pacing the floor, she laughed and replied with funny GIFs before settling again to work.

"Reminder. You have packing on today's agenda," Scarlett's staccato voice announced.

"I know, but I still have a lot of work to do." Realizing she spoke aloud to a phone that would not talk back, she shook her head and sat at the desk.

Concentrating was impossible. Each time she clicked on an image of a house to include on the landing page for *Meadow Ridge Real Estate Agency*, she thought about Luke. Kennedy recalled the conversations they shared over the past weeks and couldn't suppress a smile. She felt happy and relaxed with him and now miserable without him. The thought of his kisses were constant distractions. This deep connection was new, but she knew this was what she waited for and now couldn't fathom connecting with anyone else. She loved how well they got along. The only disconnect was about Meadow Ridge. She still imagined moving back to California but was beginning to wonder why.

The other night, Luke broached the subject again and admitted to feeling at home there and was entertaining the idea of accepting an offer to work permanently at Brian's company.

At first, Kennedy was surprised but saw in his eyes how much he liked feeling essential. She wanted that for him and later allowed her mind to imagine living permanently in Meadow Ridge. The vision didn't scare her as she originally feared.

Thoughts of Luke turned to the ache of missing him. The tightness in her chest made her want to call him, but she didn't want to be a bother while he was with his family. Navigating the distance, the holiday, and family would be tricky. Kennedy admitted defeat by closing her laptop and lifting her arms to stretch.

Ping. Her phone illuminated, and she gasped.

A tap of the screen produced a photo of Luke and his grandmother sharing a golf cart. From the angle, it appeared Gram snapped the photo with his phone.

Luke wasn't exactly smiling. His mouth was a

perfect circle, and his eyes bulged as if in shock.

Curious, Kennedy zoomed in over his eyes to check their color. Today, they appeared as green as the course they played. Would they turn blue by the pool? She chuckled and hovered a finger over the photo and meant to select the thumbs-up to indicate she liked the photo. By mistake, she tapped the heart icon alerting love, instead.

"Oops." Kennedy placed her phone screen-side down on the table. Heat crept up her neck. No ding. No buzz. No reply. *Is Luke flipping out? Did his grandmother see the heart? I only meant I love the photo, not him. Well, maybe I do? This is not the way to tell him—or his grandmother. Ugh, now I do want a response!*

Buzz. Finally, her phone lit. She grabbed it. The notification indicated a video was sent. Bracing herself, she tapped the Play button.

A striking, older woman appeared on the screen waving off-center. "Hi, dear! This is Sylvia, Luke's Gram. I am currently beating your boyfriend by six strokes. Merry Christmas!" The video ended with a shaky scene of the course.

Sighing with relief, Kennedy replayed the video until she heard the ping of an incoming text.

—Apologies!! Gram keeps taking my phone. I'll call you later!!—

Kennedy burst out laughing and replied.

—All good.—

As her heart rate returned to normal, she wondered if Gram's label would prompt a discussion on relationship status. After her appetite returned, she ate a forgettable dinner, wrapped up work, watered the tree, and retreated upstairs for the night to pack and get to bed early. Keeping busy helped to avoid overthinking what would be discussed during the call with Luke.

Once the combination of shorts and light sweaters were packed for the unpredictable weather of Naples in December, Kennedy climbed into bed and opened her laptop to peruse the last-minute Christmas deals for the few gifts still on her list. Earlier, she dropped off a thank-you basket to Lexi, and she would give Caleb a hefty transfer of money when she returned. He agreed to water the tree and generally oversee the house while she was gone.

"Don't go throwing any wild teenage parties." She had shown him the code to enter the back door when he stopped by yesterday.

"Right." He rolled his eyes. "On this block? The neighbors would call my parents before I could crack a beer."

Kennedy had laughed along with him at the time, but she sympathized with Caleb. He was a good kid and probably lived by some strict rules growing up on Poppy Lane. The parents around here seemed to be doing a good job of raising polite and responsible kids. So far, all the children she met greeted her with big waves and smiles.

She scrolled and clicked through her mother's favorite stores, selecting a few items and shipping them directly to their house. Shopping for her dad was easy. Months ago, Kennedy reordered his favorite steak subscription and purchased fishing lures. Shopping passed the time, but not as quickly as she hoped while waiting.

Ding. "Call from Luke," Scarlett announced.

Kennedy grabbed her phone and noticed the time. "Geez," she answered. "I thought old people went to bed early. It's after eleven."

Luke chuckled. "We finally finished watching the third, made-for-TV Christmas movie of the night. Gram is on a mission to watch each one before Christmas Eve, and she's bringing me down with her."

"Ha." Kennedy closed her laptop with a satisfying snap. "I watched the one about the professional skater and the farm team hockey player."

"That was Gram's favorite." Luke chuckled.

Now or never. Well, maybe not never. But here goes. "So, Gram is something else." She awaited his response with tightly shut eyes.

"Yeah, um, she says whatever is on her mind. I didn't exactly say you were my girlfriend. She assumed when I was telling her about you."

"I see." Kennedy held her breath. While she wished he'd elaborate, simply hearing he told his grandmother about her gave her hope.

"So, are you all packed and ready for your version of this?"

Kennedy released her breath. They would not be defining the relationship tonight. She shook off the regret and told herself the discussion would be better in person anyway. Easier over the phone, but more mature discussed face-to-face. Muting the microphone, she cleared her throat and summoned her happy voice to mask her disappointment before responding. "Yes, my flight is at noon. Caleb will drive me to the airport. My trip is funding his gas money for the next few months."

"Cool. What's the plan when you arrive? If your family is anything like mine, they'll have an agenda."

"Of course. Dinner is at five thirty at their community clubhouse. I think I heard something about Christmas-themed trivia afterward. They've become very activity-oriented people since retiring."

"Sounds like fun."

"Ha. Maybe I'll win and run away to join the amateur trivia tour. I'll let you know."

By the time she tapped *End Call* an hour later, Kennedy felt less lonely and more in love. Still grasping her phone as if it tethered her to him, she scrolled through recent photos. She selected the photo of Luke and Gram, saved the original, then edited a copy to display only Luke. Zooming in on his face, she cropped the image so it focused on his green eyes. Feeling like a teenager tucking the school photo of her crush into her wallet, she laughed out loud. *Oh well.* She drifted off to sleep hearing the voice of Luke's grandmother calling him her boyfriend.

The next day, Kennedy shuffled through the deplaning crowd. "Hey, Scarlett. Text Luke 'Landed,' and change the setting from airplane mode to normal and from silent to ringer on." A minute later, while descending the escalator toward baggage claim, she heard the text alert and had to suppress a squeal.

—Welcome to the sunshine state. Smile—

She replied with the smiley-face and sun emojis and happily waited for the carousel to deliver her rolling suitcase. *At least, we're back in the same state.* No one could mistake her location. Signs welcoming tourists to Florida and advertisements for retirement communities filled the baggage claim area. The air-conditioning blasted, and Kennedy was glad to exit the revolving door and feel the warm air.

Her parents waited outside the terminal and talked nonstop during the drive to their gated community. At the ranch-style house, Kennedy's dad, Rob, took her bag and retreated to a back bedroom.

A tug on her elbow prevented Kennedy from following him.

"I'm dying to ask you a million questions," Ellen said. "But we don't have a ton of time right now. Go change into resort wear for dinner and trivia." She released her grip.

"Okay, Mom." Kennedy walked toward the guest bedroom. Unsure what resort wear meant, Kennedy stepped into a floral, maxi sundress and joined her parents in their golf cart. The short drive brought them to a Spanish-style building next to the pool and tennis courts. The clubhouse not only served lunch and dinner but operated as a meeting place, bar and lounge, and recreation center for the retirement community. Kennedy understood why her parents spent a great deal of time there and as they entered, it appeared they knew everyone.

Dinner was fun and delicious. Mai tais and mahi-mahi followed by Key Lime pie sure beat her microwaved meals-for-one and take-out from the strip mall. Kennedy braced herself for the interrogation about life on Poppy Lane and Luke, but halfway through their meals, she still avoided the hot seat. She hoped Ellen was saving the questions for the "girl time" she asked Kennedy to reserve for the next afternoon.

After dinner, their dishes were cleared, and the white tablecloth was swapped for fresh, green linens. Coffee cups and wineglasses were set before them.

"See, we're fun." Ellen pointed toward the bottles

of wine at the center of the table.

Rob and Ellen were in their element, and she loved seeing them so happy. They always had fun together, and the couple who joined them to form their trivia team created a perfect match. Before the game began, the Morans introduced themselves. Deb and Dave were just a few years older than the Moores, originally from the Midwest, and thrilled to hear about Kennedy's move to Meadow Ridge.

Kennedy resisted making the correction and listened to tales of block parties and Easter egg hunts.

In between rounds of trivia, plenty of socializing occurred. Most people stood to stretch or visit the bar or bathroom. The Morans took every opportunity to gush about the upcoming visit by their daughter, son-in-law, and young grandchildren.

"We're taking the kids to the pool every morning and to the beach every day at sunset. Wednesday, we're going to the zoo." Deb beamed.

"Gonna rent a pontoon boat." Dave raised his beer bottle.

Ellen turned toward Kennedy with tight lips.

Hoping to skirt the questions about settling down, Kennedy nodded and smiled. When the next category of trivia questions was announced, she was relieved.

During the trivia match's quiet "Thinking Time," Scarlett announced a call from Luke.

Kennedy froze. Her phone was in her bag hanging over the back of the chair, and she fumbled to retrieve it before the second alert. She was a second too late. Convinced the whole room was looking at her, she rushed to the hallway. "Hi." She breathed the word.

"Wow," Luke replied. "Where did I catch you?"

"Trivia. It's getting heated in there." She kept her voice low.

He chuckled. "I won't keep you. Go have fun. Good luck and call me whenever."

Nervous, she glanced around the space to determine if she could speak louder. "I really want to talk, but I should get back. They need me."

"I want to talk, too. Anything in particular?"

"No." She held back her true feelings. She wanted to hear his intention first before spilling her heart. "Nothing special."

"Same here, but you know, I've gotten used to talking to you every night."

Kennedy's breath caught. *It's like he's reading my thoughts.* She closed her eyes. "Me, too. I look forward to it all day." She heard him sigh as if relieved. "Goodnight, Luke." She ended the call and floated back inside.

Their team advanced to the final round and took second place. The prize was a bottle of Merlot. Kennedy blushed as she carried it to the golf cart, remembering the last night she'd enjoyed that type of wine.

After church on Sunday morning, she texted Luke from her dad's car.

—Last-minute shopping with Dad—

—Same!—

—Lol. Dads!—

Spent from walking the outdoor mall with Rob and ready to relax by the pool, she stopped in her tracks when she remembered Luke's Christmas gift. "Dad, I need to pick up one quick thing. You can go to the car and wait. You look tired."

He laughed and, with a jingle, pulled the keys from his pocket. "No worries. Get something nice for your new boyfriend. Mom told me. Scarlett, too."

Kennedy rolled her eyes and groaned. Entering the sporting goods store, she crossed her fingers in hopes they carried winter sports equipment. Last week, she sneaked out to the mudroom and peeked into Luke's boot to learn his shoe size. As soon as Kennedy returned to Rob's car, she knocked on his window and indicated for him to lower it. "Pop the trunk and don't ask."

Rob nodded and obliged.

After stowing the bag containing Luke's ice skates, she slipped into the passenger seat. "So, how's your golf game these days?"

He chuckled. "Nice diversion, but I can always talk about my game. I'm trying to correct my slice, but my putting has improved." Back at the house, Rob beelined for the pool.

Through the wall of windows, Kennedy watched him fumble onto a float and place a hat over his face.

"Girl time," Ellen announced. "Let's bake."

Kennedy could not recall her mom ever baking. "Really? Since when do you bake? You were the mom who brought cupcakes from the grocery store to my school's bake sales."

"I know, but it seems like everyone else does. Plus, I want to make something to bring to tomorrow night's Christmas Eve party." Ellen tied an apron around her waist and pointed to a hook where another apron hung.

"Fine." Kennedy plucked the apron from the hook and turned toward the butcher block island. Familiar ingredients filled the countertop. "No, wait! Not snowballs."

Ellen raised an eyebrow. "Why not? Aunt Maggie was famous for them."

Kennedy lifted both eyebrows in return. "So I recently discovered. That would have been nice to know. She clearly didn't pass her talent on."

"But she passed on the recipe." Ellen cocked an eyebrow.

"No, she didn't. I found one online. I made them, but they were a disaster. I forgot to tell you the host didn't even display them. The cookies she brought from the other bakers the next day were works of art."

"You didn't have her recipe? How? Oh, Kennedy." Ellen shook her head. "Did you unpack all those boxes yet?"

She sighed. "Not exactly."

"That explains it. When you get back, find the recipe. There must be a book or a box somewhere." She shook a finger. "Your phone doesn't know everything."

Ugh. Why is she pushing me? She must really want me to unpack and commit to settling into the house. "Fine. But for now, can we please just make sugar cookies? My snowballs have an even smaller chance here in the sun."

"Deal, but the tradeoff is information." Ellen placed both hands on Kennedy's shoulders. "Spill it."

Here we go. I got this. "Okay. Meadow Ridge is perfectly fine. Sure, it is cold, but it's Indiana, not Alaska, and will get warmer. I don't know. I guess if I was older and married with kids, I would enjoy the neighborhood more. But I'm not, so I'll be back in California by next Christmas." *Will I though? This rehearsed speech no longer feels genuine and more like a defense.*

Ellen frowned and dropped her hands. "Give it time. A lot could change in a few months, and I don't only mean the weather."

"Maybe." As usual, Ellen was right. In the few weeks since Kennedy moved, a great deal already changed. She recalled Luke asking her just the other day to give Meadow Ridge a chance and stop being so stubborn about going back. With little hesitation, she agreed. She didn't want to jeopardize her connection with Luke and promised herself to give the Midwest, and maybe love, a chance. The conversation brought a smile to her face, and as she recalled the kissing that followed, her cheeks burned.

"Hello? Earth to Ken." Ellen snapped her fingers. "Please continue."

"As for Luke." Kennedy sighed. "He's everything I could ask for—thoughtful, fun, and a good listener. We're about the same age, which is nice. He has a great career, he's close with his family, and yes—since you'll ask—he's very attractive." Kennedy shuffled her feet.

Ellen stuck both hands on her hips. "Oh my gosh. You're in love."

"What? No." Sensing a blush forming, she glanced away. "Maybe. I don't know."

"Right." Ellen winked and whistled a sappy love song.

Yup, she saw right through me. Why did I think I could hide my feelings? I know I can be honest, but I just wanted to make sure this is the real deal before I gushed to Mom. Clearly, I think Luke and I have the real thing, and now she knows, too.

****

The next night, Kennedy leaned against a palm tree outside of the clubhouse. She bent her head over the phone. "The party is nice, but I needed some air." With the hand not holding her phone, she pulled her gauzy cardigan tightly around the new, sleeveless dress. Since sunset, the air cooled but remained comfortable. Something chirped with a pleasant rhythm. *Crickets? Tree frogs?* Kennedy didn't know but enjoyed their serenade.

"I hear ya. We're at Gram's brother's house, and the TV is set to the loudest level possible. I'm hiding in a bedroom."

"If one more person at the party asks why I'm not settled down yet…"

Luke snickered. "I fake cough every time. Gram must think I have bronchitis."

"Or she sees right through you." Kennedy fiddled with the charm on her necklace.

"Probably!"

A silence followed, then Kennedy heard Luke clear his throat.

"About last night. I had something I wanted to say. Something I should have said."

Oh no. Her stomach tightened into a hard ball. He sounded nervous. *Is this over? Will he say they should slow down or see other people when they got back? Am I giving him unreliable vibes by still talking about California? Did Gram not like my reply? Ugh!* "Okay. Whatever you have to say, I can take it." She clutched the phone.

Luke laughed softly. "I miss you, Kennedy. I can't stop thinking about you."

Her stomach unclenched, and butterflies took over.

I'm so dumb. We have a good thing. I want this, him, and better voice my feelings now. "I miss you, too." She turned her gaze toward the night sky and smiled with pure joy. "I knew I would, but I didn't realize how much until you left."

"As soon as I got here, I realized I didn't want to be away from you," Luke said.

A tightness gripped her throat, but a lightness washed over her. "I'm right there with you."

"I wish you really were here with me. I want to hold you," Luke said.

Kennedy closed her eyes and imagined his arms holding her close. "I can't wait to see you and feel you hold me again. I hope Santa is good to you tonight." She didn't want to risk saying anything else and ruining the warm feeling.

"I don't need Santa this Christmas; I only need you, Kennedy."

"You've got me," she whispered. Her throat felt tight, but she was glad she spoke quietly. This moment felt private, despite the public location. Two men laughed and smoked cigars in nearby lawn chairs. "I wish I could say more, but I'm not exactly alone."

"That's all I need to hear. I'd better get back to the relatives. Merry Christmas, Kennedy."

"Merry Christmas, Luke. Enjoy the evening with your family." Kennedy choked back tears and stayed outside replaying Luke's words in her head before rejoining the party. Feeling like she held a top-level secret, Kennedy found focusing difficult. She picked at appetizers and chatted with her family and their friends in Naples, but her mind was in Miami.

After Christmas dinner the following afternoon,

Kennedy video chatted with Luke. She was so happy to finally see his smile, not just hear his voice. Upon request, she displayed the Christmas gifts from her parents. Sweaters, a down vest, shearling boots, and a car ice scraper were among Kennedy's gifts.

Luke received a gray sweater, matching wool socks, a frying pan, and a car ice scraper.

"I detect a theme," she said.

"An obvious theme from the southerners." Luke waggled his brows.

"I have a gift for you that fits right in. I can't wait to see you open it when we're home." Kennedy immediately realized she said "we" and "home" in the same sentence and hoped he didn't read into it. Then again, they made progress with sharing their feelings last night. Still, she clenched her jaw.

"Awesome. I'll be back Thursday since my parents set sail the next day for the Caribbean. You're not back until Saturday, right? I know you'll be tired and all, but I can't wait to see you again. Can I come over that night?"

Kennedy released her held breath. "Absolutely. I'm supposed to fly the next day to California for my friend's New Year's Eve party."

"Oh, right." His smile faded, and he dropped his gaze.

Is he sad? Will he miss me? What will he do instead? The thought of being away from him tightened her stomach. "Come with me!"

Luke raised his head. As he lifted his hands into view, his eyes widened. "What?"

"Seriously. All my friends have someone, and I dreaded going alone." She raised a hand to face the screen. "No, wait, I didn't mean it like that. You totally shouldn't feel guilted into coming. I just, um, really want you there." Kennedy stopped talking to avoid blowing her chance. Off screen, she gripped the edge of the table and waited for his reply. *This is a long shot. I shouldn't get my hopes up, especially after that less-than-eloquent offer.*

Chuckling, Luke shook his head. "Kennedy, relax. I'd love to go. I want to be with you, too. I meant what I said last night. I don't want to have this missing-you sensation again. In fact, let's make the arrangements now. Get Scarlett to work. She's had enough vacation."

The next day, Kennedy texted her group of friends about the new plan. Instead of her original arrangement of sleeping on Becca's couch, she and Luke would be staying at the only hotel in the area with rooms available over the holiday. She hit Send and waited for the onslaught of replies. Two minutes later, her phone illuminated.

—Can't wait to meet the man—

—Luke is gonna be initiated—

—Did you get a room at the Luxe?—

As excited as she was for her friends to meet Luke, she worried about the annual party at Tiffany's penthouse. The event was formal and sparkly, fun but snooty. Tiffany went over-the-top with everything, and New Year's Eve was her time to shine. Usually one drama-filled argument ensued, and someone always got too drunk, but every year they dressed up and pretended like everything would be perfect. *Ugh, what am I getting us into?* What felt like a good idea yesterday was now stressful. She wanted to be alone with Luke. How could she finagle more time? Kennedy hatched another idea. "Hey, Scarlett?"

****

Thursday

"Mom." Kennedy rose from the chaise lounge and pulled on her cover-up. "I'm going inside for more sunblock. Do you need anything?"

With both hands, Ellen shielded her eyes and squinted. "No, thanks. I'm good. I might even jump in the pool while you're gone and can't criticize my doggie paddle."

"At least you get in and try." Kennedy laughed and opened the sliding door. She walked through the kitchen and pulled her phone from the pocket of the terry cloth jumper.

—You back?—

—Just getting a ride-share to my condo. Miss you—

—Me too. I hope you miss me enough to do me a big favor—

Kennedy hit Send and tensed. White dots indicated he was typing.

—Of course. Anything—

—Thanks! Can you go to my house around noon tomorrow? I have a delivery arriving, and someone needs to sign. Caleb's not 18 yet—

—Sure. Use code at back door?—

—Yes. I owe you one—

Feeling excited, but still craving encouragement, Kennedy closed the messaging app and opened her photo folder. She tapped on the photo of Luke. Yup, one look at those eyes and she knew she was doing the right thing.

****

Friday

Forcing a wide smile, Kennedy turned to face her mother who, so far, remained silent for the forty-five-minute drive. "I had a great time, Mom. I really did. I just need to get back to reset before flying out west. You know, I have a house to check on now." *I'll miss Mom and Dad, but this decision feels right. I've never wanted a vacation to end early. Luke better be happy to see me.*

Ellen sighed. "I guess I understand, and it's only a day earlier than I expected." With a forced smile, she hugged Kennedy at the Fort Myers airport.

"Have a Happy New Year, Mom."

"Call me!" Ellen blew a kiss.

Kennedy felt evil at the time, but now as the car approached Poppy Lane, she was glad for taking the chance at pulling off this surprise. Pointing toward Caleb's house, she asked the driver to pull over. The frigid air smacked her cheeks, and she regretted not packing her coat. The long, black cardigan was stylish but no match for the January temperature. At the sight of Luke's silver car parked in her driveway, she sped her pace, dragging her suitcase over the icy sidewalk and bumping it up the front steps. Giddiness overtook her as she rang the bell. She intended to hide her excitement, but when she heard Luke announce he was coming, she lost all composure.

Luke opened the door, and his jaw dropped.

"Surprise! I'm the delivery." She flung wide her arms.

Luke picked up Kennedy by the waist and spun her into the house. "This is the best surprise I ever got." He leaned in and kissed her forehead. "You, Kennedy, are the best surprise in my life. I've never been so happy."

Tears pooled. She wrapped her arms around his neck and inhaled his comforting, musky scent. "I wish I could come up with some original words, but I feel the exact same way."

"Hearing my feelings returned are the best words I could ever hope to hear." He hugged her again, then lowered his head. "I only fear losing you to California. I told myself to hold back because you're not here to stay. But I can't anymore. I've fallen in love with you, and if that means I have to move again, I will."

The tears previously threatening now spilled over as Kennedy smiled. "Oh, Luke. Now I can't stop these happy tears. We'll find a solution. I promise I'll give Poppy Lane more of a chance because I'm in love with you, too. She tightened her embrace and felt her anxiety melt away as his hands caressed her back. *Forget worrying about relationship labels. This is the real thing. I am totally in love.*

After a moment, Luke released his grip and placed his hands on Kennedy's shoulders. "I hate to tell you this, but I have to get back to the office." He winced.

Kennedy slapped a palm to her forehead. "No! I'm so sorry I forgot. You thought you were only meeting the delivery guy. Is it your lunch break? Let me find you something."

"Relax." Luke grasped her hands. "I already ate on the way here, but I have a meeting until six. Can I bring dinner after?"

"I'd love that." In the doorway, Kennedy kissed him goodbye and retreated to the house. She exhaled a loud sigh and plopped on the couch. *I'm in love. Stick a fork in me, I'm done.* After several minutes of mentally replaying his words, she yawned. Worried about pulling off this surprise, she hadn't slept a wink the night before. Now that the surprise was a success, more than a success, she fell into a peaceful nap.

The next morning was Saturday, and Luke returned with a bag full of ingredients for making breakfast. Turkey bacon sizzled on a pan and eggs sat in a glass bowl, waiting to be cracked. On an electric skillet, Luke flipped golden, fluffy pancakes. Despite the vent set to the highest setting and rattling the windows, the bacon's salty aroma overwhelmed the small space.

Holding aloft her phone, Kennedy walked into the kitchen. "Hey, Scarlett, what time does the closest skating rink open today?"

"The Meadow Ridge Park District rink is open today, Saturday, December twenty-ninth, from ten am until sunset. Sunset will occur at four thirty-two."

"Okay, fine." Luke threw both hands in the air.

"You'll love it. I'll teach you all my tricks." She stretched to tiptoe and kissed his cheek.

"Just teach me not to fall." Luke opened his gift the night before and though he regretted telling her weeks ago that he'd never ice-skated, he swore to try.

At two, Kennedy sat on a green, park bench and leaned over to unlace her skates. As she pulled on her boots, the first snowflakes fell.

From the seat beside Kennedy, Luke turned his face to the darkening sky. "Huh."

"Is it supposed to snow?" Kennedy asked.

The woman seated to the other side of Kennedy whipped her head. "Really? You're not aware we're getting a huge storm tonight? It's supposed to snow through Sunday. It's been all over the news. Where have you been?"

"Um, Florida." Kennedy winced and turned away.

Luke shrugged. "I had no idea. I guess we've been distracted." He smirked.

Kennedy grinned.

By the time they inched onto Poppy Lane, the visibility was low. A measurable amount of snow already accumulated. Once inside and sharing a blanket and cups of tea on the couch, Luke turned to Kennedy. "Are you thinking what I'm thinking?"

"Yup." Kennedy lifted her phone. "Hey, Scarlett, what's the forecast?"

"Tonight, there is a winter storm advisory for the area. Up to a foot of snow is expected overnight before turning to freezing rain mixed with snow by Sunday morning."

"Yikes," Luke said. "What do you think the chances are of our flight getting out tomorrow?"

Kennedy scrunched her eyes. "About a snowball's chance."

That night, Luke and Kennedy made a makeshift dinner with the leftover eggs and turkey bacon and never discussed Luke staying over. The wind howled while snow whipped sideways. The road was last visible hours ago. In no way could he drive home. The sleepover conversation was dodged by staying up all night watching documentaries in the living room.

After midnight, Kennedy was engrossed in an expose of a pop singer from her high school days when she detected a shift in Luke's breathing. She lowered the volume as the documentary ended with a montage of the famous music videos and hesitated a moment to ensure he was asleep before moving. Raising the remote, she clicked off the TV and tucked the blanket tighter. "I could do this forever," she whispered.

The corners of Luke's mouth turned up.

Afraid to ruin the moment, Kennedy clasped her hands to resist touching Luke. She yearned to snuggle but settled for the closeness and shut her eyes. *I have no need to rush. I am so appreciative for finding him and this love. We've joked about karma being responsible, but I know who I really need to thank. Yes, Aunt Maggie, you were right, and I've never been so happy to be wrong.*

Chapter Eight

The morning sun shone brightly and reflected harshly off the ice-encrusted snow. Sunday had been a mess with the storm first dumping snow, then pelting ice, and finally delivering rain. Now, on Monday, Kennedy and Luke stood at the kitchen sink, each gripping a mug and assessing the storm's damage. The power went out twice overnight, but thankfully it was restored in time to brew coffee. Hazelnut-flavored pods were all that remained, and the nutty aroma filled the room. "I don't know where to start." Kennedy pointed at the window.

Shaking his head, Luke reached over the faucet and lowered the window's blind. He turned to face Kennedy and grinned. "No rush. It's New Year's Eve. Neither of us has anywhere to go today. I wish I had my laptop so I could get a half-day's work done, but maybe I can manage with my phone and your tablet. Brian's product goes live on Wednesday, so I need to send a few blasts."

"Right, this is the big week. Please use whatever you need." Kennedy patted Luke's arm.

"Thanks. I say we leave the snow until the sun melts the coating of ice." He pulled out a kitchen chair. "Sit down and enjoy the beautiful morning."

The smile creeping across her face was too obvious to conceal. *Why bother*? Before this weekend, she hid her feelings, but now, well, the vibe felt different—hopeful. The last two nights had been wonderful. Luke had no choice but to stay a second night as the storm never let up. With the roads so treacherous, she wouldn't have let him go anyway. Watching movies, drinking wine, and eating stale Christmas cookies filled the days and nights. Kennedy never experienced such a deep connection with anyone and held little doubt she'd found the real thing with Luke.

On Sunday, she had texted her friends in California about the change of plans. Feigning disappointment at missing the party, she promised to bring Luke to visit soon and sent a photo of Poppy Lane covered in snow and ice.

Her friends thought it looked like a nightmare.

To play along, Kennedy laughed but secretly felt like she was living in a dream. Now, she hated to ask but bit the bullet. "Besides a little work, what shall we do today?"

Luke grinned and kept his gaze fixed on his coffee mug. "I have an idea, but I don't want to pressure you." He twirled the mug.

Kennedy's heart began to pound. "Oh?"

Luke chuckled and lifted his head.

She raised an eyebrow. "Elaborate, please."

"Nothing terrible. Nothing naughty. Well, um, how do you feel about settling down?"

"What?" Kennedy knocked over her coffee cup.

With a gasp, Luke jumped, grabbed a napkin, and blotted the spill. "Wow! You should see your expression. Sorry. Allow me to rephrase. How about unpacking the boxes today? I think you'll feel better about the house. Your house. I think the presence of the boxes is holding you back. I'm happy to help, but only if you want."

Kennedy was silent for a minute. She strummed her fingers on the wooden table as her heart rate slowly returned to a normal pace. He was only asking her to unpack, she reminded herself. The thought of settling down scared her only a few weeks before, but now the fear disappeared. Realizing the feeling was excitement, not dread, she reached across the table for his hand. *I love him. Nothing feels overwhelming anymore. He just caught me off guard.* "Sounds like a good idea, and I do want to find her recipe."

Luke squeezed her hand. "Think of it as an experiment. Maybe unpacking the boxes will unpack some feelings, too."

"I'll give it a shot." She grinned.

By two p.m., all the boxes were inspected and sorted. One box was designated for donations. Kennedy carefully placed Aunt Maggie's clothes and knickknacks in a box and sealed the top with tape. She liked to think Maggie would be happy she was taking steps towards embracing the house. Kennedy carried a box of mementos to the attic. Earlier, she found drawers and closets for everything worth keeping. She had to admit the house was beginning to look like a home.

****

Luke broke down the empty boxes that once held kitchen utensils, linens, and towels He carried the flattened cardboard to the garage. Curious about the amount of snowfall, he pushed the wall-mounted button to raise the garage door. As the hinges creaked, Luke spied the legs, then torso, and finally the whole of body of a teenage boy. "You must be Caleb." Luke walked closer and extended a hand.

Caleb stepped into the garage and shook. "Yeah. I came to see if Ms. Moore wants her driveway and walk cleared."

"I'll go ask. I'm Luke, by the way."

"I know." Caleb grinned.

Luke returned to the house and found Kennedy in the kitchen. "Raise the blind and let your buddy know if you want the snow cleared." He pointed toward the window over the sink.

"Great." Kennedy pulled the cord, allowing light to flood the room, waved to Caleb, and offered a thumbs-up.

****

While Caleb used his new snowblower outside her house, Kennedy made hot cocoa. *Shoot. I should probably start buying marshmallows and snacks to have on hand. I'll bet Caleb gets a better reception at the other houses on the block.*

Luke met Kennedy in the kitchen. "Caleb seems like a good kid."

"He's been such a help. He's very reliable and friendly. Most of the kids I met so far on the block seem really nice and well-mannered."

"Another plus for Poppy Lane?" Luke grinned.

"Yeah, I guess so." Kennedy nodded and offered a mug. "Speaking of the street, my car is no longer trapped, but yours got buried by the plows passing by. Do you need a ride to your condo?" Hoping the answer was no, she crossed her fingers.

"Are you kicking me out?" Luke grinned and raised his mug.

Shaking her head, Kennedy searched for the right

words to convey here true feelings. *Please stay!* screamed in her head, but she knew it would sound too forceful. "I hate to presume you want to stay again, and I don't want to make you feel trapped. But we would've been in San Francisco together tonight, so I hope you still want to be with me." She wrung her hands.

Luke clasped her twitching hands and stared into her eyes. He wrapped his arms around Kennedy and planted a kiss on the top of her head before retuning his gaze. "I don't feel trapped. I'm happy to be stuck with you. Just because our view is snowy instead of sandy doesn't mean plans have changed."

"Nor to me." Kennedy felt tears brim and raised her chin.

"I can't think of anywhere else I'd rather be than with you." Luke pulled in Kennedy tightly to his chest.

She breathed in his now-familiar scent and sighed. "This is the only place I want to be tonight. After spending the last few days with you and unpacking, I already feel more connected to the house. And, of course, you."

Luke loosened his embrace and met her gaze. "I'm so happy to hear you say those words. That's reason enough to celebrate. We don't need a party. We only need each other and maybe some champagne."

"Ooh, that I don't have." Kennedy shook her head. "Or any groceries. I had few to begin with and dwindled my reserves before I left for Florida. Now, with the storm, the cupboard is totally bare."

He dropped his arms and donned a wide grin. "Leave it to me. If I can take your car, I'll search for an open store and get whatever I can find to make a special dinner. I wouldn't mind stopping at my place for a change of clothes and to make sure the heat is on and all that stuff. I'll dig out my car tomorrow."

"Perfect. I could use a shower, and I'll finish picking up while you're gone."

After a long, hot shower where Kennedy sang sappy love songs and laughed at how giddy she felt, an idea formed. One of her aunt's boxes was filled with china and crystal. Initially, she considered leaving the items in the box but instead stacked them on the dining room table with the intent of eventually filling the china cabinet. The antique cabinet was not Kennedy's style, but the ornate piece belonged in the space. Now, she conjured a better plan than simply leaving the formal dining ware to collect dust in the unused room. Tonight, she would create a five-star restaurant. She pulled out her phone.

—Take your time—

—I was hoping you'd ask me to rush back—

—LOL. I'm working on something. You'll see—

Scarlett advised Kennedy of the proper layout for formal dining. She draped a tablecloth over the oval, black walnut table and arranged matching napkins. Two ivory-and-gold china plates now sat between heirloom silverware. Crystal water and wineglasses and champagne flutes sparkled at the top of each setting.

"Candles." Kennedy snapped her fingers. She rummaged again through the china cabinet and discovered two tapers to insert into the candlesticks she found earlier in the top drawer. "Perfect."

"Yes," Luke said.

"Ah!" She jumped and placed a hand over her racing heart. "Oh my gosh. I didn't hear you arrive."

From behind her, Luke wrapped his arms around

her waist and kissed her neck. "That was the plan. I wanted to see what you were up to. The table looks great."

Entwining her fingers with his, she then leaned back and tilted her head to invite more kisses. "Everything feels right," she murmured.

"Almost." Luke leaned to his left and caused a rustle. "Please ask Scarlett how to cook lobsters." He held up a plastic bag and grinned.

The cuckoo clock mounted on the dining room wall indicated ten o'clock when they finished dinner. Luke disappeared to the kitchen and returned carrying two pieces of cherry-topped cheesecake on paper plates. "I don't know if you like cheesecake, but it was all they had left. Unless you want leftover cookies."

Kennedy clasped her hands. "I love it, but that reminds me we never found my aunt's recipe for snowballs."

"You're right." Luke slid his fork into the creamy dessert. "We went through everything. I'm sorry. I hoped you'd find it, too."

Kennedy shrugged. "Maybe it's for the best. I could never do justice to her recipe." She took a large bite and smirked. While lingering at the table, Kennedy shared stories of past New Year's Eve celebrations and disasters.

"Everyone hypes up the evening, but I think the whole thing is overrated. When the night finally ends, I usually end up disappointed. I don't think I'll feel that way tonight."

Kennedy tilted her head. "Midnight is nearing and so far, so good this year."

"One more element is necessary." Luke blew out

the candles, then pushed back his chair, pulled out Kennedy's chair, and led her to the living room. The tree still stood, and the tiny lights reflected off the bay window. Its needles hung on, but the branches drooped. "Close your eyes. I'll be right back."

A now-familiar flutter stirred in her stomach. Love, not fear. She clenched her fists and listened for Luke's return. Seconds away from him felt like an eternity. *What could he possibly be doing now? Whatever it is, I'm ready. I'm ready to settle, move, whatever it takes to keep this blissful feeling.*

He approached slowly. "This might be the best New Year's Eve I've ever had, Kennedy. Thank you for letting me into your life." He leaned in and placed a quick kiss on her cheek. "You can look now."

Kennedy opened her eyes and saw the man she wanted to spend the rest of her life with, standing before her holding two glasses of champagne and a single white rose. Sensing this was a moment she'd want to treasure, she held her breath.

"I love you, Kennedy Moore." His voice cracked, and his eyes were wet.

Kennedy pressed her hands to cover her heart. "I love you, too." Accepting a glass and the rose, she placed one in each hand and wrapped her arms around Luke's neck and kissed him tenderly, hoping to convey her sincerity.

"You feel like home, and wherever you want to go, I'll follow. If you let me."

Her knees felt wobbly. "You are doing a pretty good job of making me feel at home here." She pointed at her heart and then the floor. "And, yes, here, too."

With a thumb, Luke wiped a tear from her cheek

and kissed the spot where tear kiss fell.

Lifting her lips, Kennedy hoped to encourage more kissing. The kiss continued until a ruckus outside ensued.

"Now what?" Luke groaned.

"Is that a chorus of trumpets?" she asked.

The unmistakable sound of party-blowers bleated.

With a sigh, Kennedy led Luke to the window.

The neighbors stood on their lawns tooting cardboard horns, flapping clackers, and even banging pots and pans.

Kennedy dropped her head to Luke's chest and laughed. "I guess we missed the countdown."

"The best one I ever missed." Luke grinned. "But, come on. Let's go join them." He threw back the flute of champagne with one hand and squeezed Kennedy with the other.

"Hang on, I need to catch up. They sound rowdy." The champagne burned as it quickly disappeared, and she struggled not to cough as she walked to the door.

Luke held out Kennedy's coat and slipped on his navy wool. They pulled on gloves and strode out to the sidewalk. The icy snow crunched underfoot.

The crowd sang the old familiar song Kennedy loved, though she never learned the words. She slipped her arm around Luke's waist and swayed her hips to the music.

Luke met her rhythm and hummed the tune.

When the song ended, the neighbors yelled, "Happy New Year," and strolled to each other offering hugs and handshakes. Kennedy and Luke greeted their new friends and listened to resolutions about eating healthy and exercising.

"Next up is the winter social," Caleb's mom, Jenny, said. "I hope you two like bowling."

"Wow, this block is very active," Kennedy said.

Jenny laughed. "We hold an event at least once a month. For Valentine's Day, we do a progressive dinner. Well, I better go find my kids and get them back inside. Happy New Year!"

"Happy New Year." Kennedy turned to Luke and widened her eyes.

"And you thought this town was slow-paced." Luke chuckled.

"I stand corrected. Now, let's make a run for it before I get talked into organizing the block party or Memorial Day barbecue." Back inside, she shrugged off her coat. "What a fun night."

"That sure beat a cover charge for two watery cocktails and a mediocre band." Luke removed his coat and hung it on the wooden peg in the mudroom. He reached for Kennedy's short, puffy jacket and hung it next to his.

Her heart swelled. He was staying. "Careful. I could get used to this."

Luke grinned. "I really hope you do."

"Hey, Scarlett. Stream romantic music to the speaker." She turned to face Luke. "Let's start this new year right."

"The first of many, I hope." Luke leaned over and turned off the lamp.

I hope forever.

Chapter Nine

The following December

"Hi, Mom," Kennedy said to the phone lying on the counter. The screen displayed a photo of Ellen wearing a straw hat and sunglasses. She wiped her flour-covered hands on a paper towel.

"How's the baking going this year?"

"Much better now that I have Aunt Maggie's recipe."

Luke shuffled closer to the phone. "And a helper!"

"Hey there, Luke," Ellen said.

Kennedy hip-bumped Luke as he measured the butter. She discovered the proper way was to slice the butter cold, not melt and pour. The cookies now had a chance.

"We're winning this year." Luke pumped his fists in the air, lifting the emerald-green apron Kennedy recently gave him. Last St. Patrick's Day, he discovered she preferred his eyes to appear green and obliged wearing the color whenever he could, even while baking.

"Well, good luck and have fun at the party. I can't wait to see you both in a couple of weeks. I still can't believe you convinced us to come there for Christmas."

"Luke's parents are equally shocked and called this

morning to ask if they need to pack snow boots. Gram, on the other hand, sent us a photo of the ice skates she bought for the trip." Kennedy recalled the image and laughed.

"I look forward to meeting her. Well, good luck with the baking and the party. I'm leaving for happy hour at the clubhouse. Bye!"

"Bye, Mom. Have fun." Kennedy wiped her palms on the Mrs. Claus apron—she now thought of it as hers as she did the house, neighborhood, and Luke. She walked to the refrigerator but hesitated before opening the newly fixed door. A magnet advertising *Meadow Ridge Real Estate Agency* held this year's invitation in place. Kennedy beamed at her work product and the paper beneath. The print on the invitation was similar to the original version she received last year, but instead of only her name penned in at the top, this year's read *Kennedy and Luke*.

"I'm glad your neighbors recognize us as a couple. The acknowledgement makes me happy, but they know I don't live here, right?"

"At the Halloween party, Marci asked me if it was correct to add your name. She said she didn't want to put 'and guest' when everyone knows we're together. I happily told her yes and then asked if the neighbors know we're not shacking up. She laughed and reminded me we're all adults."

"So, I shouldn't worry?" Luke asked.

"No. In fact, Marci said to stop caring what everyone thinks about us and just make killer cookies."

Until two days ago, she wasn't sure what type of cookies they would make. Neither she nor Luke had yet to find the so-called famous recipe, and she was losing hope they ever would. Both researched various versions and were about to try one more when Lexi had stopped by after dinner. While she dried the dishes, Kennedy heard a knock. "C'mon in!" The front door was unlocked, as it usually was these days. Kennedy quickly became accustomed to Lexi, Caleb, and other neighbors dropping in at any time. The company was always welcome, and Kennedy learned to have drinks and snacks on hand. She was also no longer embarrassed by the state of her living room. New upholstery adorned the sofas. Fun throw pillows accented the wing chairs, and hardwood floors now gleamed after being hidden for years under the wall-to-wall mauve carpet. A fluffy, soft, gray rug filled the space beneath a brass-and-glass table. Kennedy was proud of the transformation she and Luke created. She folded the dish towel, hung it on the dishwasher's handle, and met Lexi in the living room.

"I hate to interrupt," Lexi said. "But I wanted to show you the write-up in our local real estate magazine. It's no big deal, but to us in the business, it's cause for bragging rights." She thrust out a thin, glossy publication.

Adorning the cover was a full-length photo of Lexi standing in front of a gorgeous, brick house. She held a *Sold* sign and flashed a wide smile. Below the photo read *Cover story, page two.* The magazine was twelve pages long.

"Beautiful." Kennedy had not taken the photo and didn't understand the significance.

Lexi made a gesture suggesting Kennedy turn the pages.

Kennedy turned to page two and recognized the familiar heading. The banner and graphics she spent most of the previous winter creating spread across two pages. Kennedy felt her cheeks tighten with a proud smile. Her new copyright stamp was just large enough to be seen but not overwhelm.

"Do you love it?" Lexi clapped rapidly and bounced on her heels. "I love it. I received three calls today asking for your contact information. You can read the full story about me later."

"Wow." The photo was the reassurance she needed to believe her efforts were worth the hard work she invested over the last year. Her freelance business started slowly but took off over the summer. By June, she began to call Poppy Lane home. Luke never pushed, but she knew he was glad whenever she made steps toward accepting the house and Meadow Ridge. For his birthday in September, she secretly obtained her Indiana's driving license and gave him the surrendered California license to show her commitment. Her most recent step was officially resigning from Hartley Advertising. Holding the publication felt like proof of a well-made decision.

Luke walked into the room and greeted Lexi. "What's going on?"

Kennedy pointed to the magazine.

He beamed. "I knew you'd be a hit. Both of you. You work well together. I was just telling Brian the same thing at the office last week."

"You're so sweet," Lexi said. "Speaking of sweet, are you two ready for the cookie exchange? It won't be as fancy as mine last year, but Marci will do a good job."

Kennedy shuffled her feet. "Yeah, actually we're still struggling with what to make."

"Really?" Lexi crossed her arms and cocked her head. "Why?"

"We never found Maggie's recipe for the snowballs."

Lexi dropped her arms and bent over laughing.

She's laughing at my expense. What dumb mistake did I make to set her off this time? I can only imagine. Kennedy knit her eyebrows and turned toward Luke.

Luke shrugged.

"Forgive me." Lexi laid a hand on each of their shoulders. "I don't mean to laugh. The entire block, no make that the town, has the recipe."

"What?" Kennedy and Luke asked in unison.

"Every year, she would include a handwritten copy with each dozen. I have it memorized."

Ah. Now, I understand why everyone in town assumed I made good snowballs. I must have looked like a fool. I must seem like the clichéd, unaware millennial I was trying to avoid. Kennedy shook her head. "You've got to be kidding me."

"Sorry. Please don't feel bad. Maggie probably didn't have it written anywhere because she knew it so well." Lexi suddenly gasped. "Oh."

"What now?"

"The secret ingredient. Well, you got that covered." She lifted the left side of her mouth. "I gotta run, but when I get home, I'll send you a screenshot of the recipe. I know I have it somewhere." Lexi waved with both hands.

Months ago, Kennedy learned the gesture was Lexi's signature goodbye. She also learned to appreciate her neighbor and her high energy. After Lexi left, Kennedy rested her back against Luke's chest. "I can hardly wait."

"Don't worry." He wrapped his arms around Kennedy's waist. "Once we get the recipe, we'll make the best snowballs this town has ever seen or tasted. We'll make several batches, and I won't leave until we get it right. I promise."

While still in the embrace, she spun to face him. "You're the best, Luke. I don't know what I would do without you."

"I'm not going anywhere. You're stuck with me."

Stretching to tiptoes, Kennedy kissed his ear. "That's good to hear because I'm madly in love with you."

With a swift scoop, Luke had lifted her legs and carried her to the couch.

Now, Luke returned to the kitchen counter with more snowball ingredients and leaned in for a kiss.

"What was that for?" Kennedy held aloft her floury hands. Through the residue, her nails shone a festive red. Not usually a manicure kind of girl, she splurged yesterday in anticipation of the ring. Tomorrow would mark a year since their first date at the brewery. After little debate, she agreed the right time would be after the cookie exchange. Their families would arrive the following week to celebrate the engagement and plan the summer wedding. Kennedy was giddy each time she thought about the plan.

"For everything. I can't wait to spend every day with you." Luke grinned. "Hey, Scarlett. Please recite the recipe for Aunt Maggie's Christmas Snowball Cookies."

"Sure. Here is Aunt Maggie's Christmas Snowball Cookie Recipe."

Aunt Maggie's Christmas Snowball Cookie Recipe

1 cup butter, softened
1/4 cup sugar
1 teaspoon vanilla extract
2 cups all-purpose flour
2 cups finely chopped pecans
Powdered sugar
*Special Ingredient

Step One: Heat oven to 325°F

Step Two: Cream butter and sugar in a medium bowl until creamy. Add vanilla; beat until well mixed.

Step Three: Add flour and pecans; beat at low speed, scraping bowl occasionally, until well mixed.

Step Four: Shape dough into 1-inch balls. Place 1 inch apart onto ungreased cookie sheets. Bake 16-18 minutes or until very lightly browned. Cool 5 minutes; roll in powdered sugar while still warm and again when cool.

*Finally, and most importantly, add the special ingredient—love.

A word about the author…

As the mother of three girls, Ally finds creating drama for her characters an escape from the real drama in her own home. Originally from Boston, she now lives with her husband and family outside Chicago.

Other Titles by this Author

Secret Admirer

The Roast

Thank you for purchasing
this publication of The Wild Rose Press, Inc.

For questions or more information
contact us at
info@thewildrosepress.com.

The Wild Rose Press, Inc.
www.thewildrosepress.com

CPSIA information can be obtained
at www.ICGtesting.com
Printed in the USA
BVHW030832241022
650134BV00016B/403